TRUCE 4: THE FINALE

TRUCE
FOUR
THE FINALE

T. STYLES

ARE YOU ON OUR EMAIL LIST?

SIGN UP ON OUR WEBSITE

www.thecartelpublications.com

OR TEXT THE WORD: CARTELBOOKS

TO 22828

FOR PRIZES, CONTESTS, ETC.

CHECK OUT OTHER TITLES BY THE CARTEL PUBLICATIONS

By T. STYLES

4

WWW.THECARTELPUBLICATIONS.COM

TRUCE 4: THE FINALE 5

Truce 4

The Finale

By

T. STYLES

Library of Congress Control Number: 2021906774

ISBN 10: 1948373750

ISBN 13: 978-1-948373-75-3

Cover Design: Book Slut Girl

First Edition

What Up Fam,

I do hope and pray that this little love note finds you well and in good spirits. Remember to keep your heads up and try to do something that will make you smile and laugh! Laughter heals.

Moving right into the book in hand, **TRUCE 4: THE FINALE**! Mannnnnnn when I finished reading this I was at a loss for words. Not only did T. Styles take you on a journey, but she left you gagging for more! This was a 12-part series/saga, her longest running story to date and I cannot wait until it is transformed into a TV series because it DESERVES to be on the big screen! And believe me...Your mind will be blown away when you're done! But don't take my word for it...read it for yourself!

With that being said, keeping in line with tradition, we want to give respect to a vet or new trailblazer paving the way. In this novel, we would like to recognize:

DMX

Earl "DMX" Simmons is a rapper/actor and I saw him as a prophet whom we recently lost. His rhymes and cadence were of LEGENDS! Some of my greatest coming up moments had his music and movies playing in the background. I am forever grateful that he shared his gifts with the world. Rest in Heaven sir!

Aight, I ain't gonna even hold you! Go 'head and jump into this here!

Love ya'll!
God Bless!

Charisse "C. Wash" Washington
Vice President
The Cartel Publications
www.thecartelpublications.com
www.facebook.com/publishercwash
Instagram: publishercwash
www.twitter.com/cartelbooks
www.facebook.com/cartelpublications
www.theelitewritersacademy.com
Follow us on Instagram: Cartelpublications
#CartelPublications
#UrbanFiction
#PrayForCece
#RIHDMX

WAR
Series
in Order

#TRUCE4

PROLOGUE

UNHAPPILY EVER AFTER

A baby blue sky with fluffy clouds provided the perfect backdrop for the ten-million-dollar jet that glided through its center like a bowling ball on a freshly oiled lane. Inside the massive luxurious aircraft, scared to death, sat the passengers.

They smelled of foul fish, smoke, and despair.

And none of the passengers, not a one, was certain that they would make it to paradise. Besides, most of them didn't deserve the classic happily ever after. After all, some had killed.

Lied.

And even manipulated to get what they wanted.

But when I tell you karma touched each one of their lives, believe me that it did. And so, for the past twenty-four days they were hunted.

They were plucked off.

Only to realize that they would never be able to return to their birthplace ever again.

Propped in lavish seats, as they scanned one another's faces, their hearts pumped wildly inside of their chests. On the aircraft, they were the only people alive who knew what it meant to make the escape.

As a result, if someone shot down the plane it would be over for their legacies.

But it was in God's hands now.

While most knowing the odds were against them.

CHAPTER ONE

WRINKLED SHEETS

The sun's rays gently caressed Banks Wales' back as he sat at his desk wearing nothing but white silk pajama pants. Tatted to the Gods, he wrote briskly in the leather rustic brown padfolio before him inside his bedroom.

Banks, the great detailer, always made plans.

And now he was checking them twice.

It was important to him that every action went through without a hitch. Because if anything went wrong, if one detail was overlooked, he could run the risk of not successfully breaking Ace out of the facility as well as losing what he had come to cherish again.

His family.

Banks was definitely back.

After Mason was shot by Jersey, a month earlier, he experienced a flood of thoughts that he learned were actual recollections of the past. With these echoes came emotions and suddenly the immense need to protect his children. Even the older ones who felt they were out of the scope of his security.

But he was Banks Wales.

Someone who would do what he needed even if it be against their will.

"Banks," a woman called from the mountain of wrinkled white sheets in the center of his bed.

He looked back at the yellow beauty in utter irritation.

"I want some more." She moaned before taking her two fingers and gliding them between her lips and deeply inside of her pussy. When they glistened, she licked them clean.

Shorty was sexy as fuck the night before.

But now it was giving, well, slut.

He focused back on his desk. "I'm busy." He looked at her again. "On second thought, get out."

With that the door opened and two men entered on a mission. They always heard what he needed, even if he didn't think they were listening.

One of them, Munro, tossed her over his shoulder and carried her toward the exit. Her long black hair brushed against his back until she was out of sight. Within seconds, the door shut, and calmness was restored.

Ah...silence.

With her out of his bed, Banks again went over the plans.

THE LIST

Secure the jet

Purchase suitcases for cash stacks

Liquidate all small businesses

Bump up security for family

Ensure the safety of:

Blakeslee, Walid, Minnesota, Joey/Sidney,

Spacey/Riot, Shay/Patrick

Check safe house

Get Ace legally (Plan A)

Get Ace out illegally (Plan B)

Fly to island

He reviewed the list five more times until an hour passed and he was pleased.

Banks looked at his older children as they sat around a boardroom table. He felt immense pride at seeing the Wales family from up under the gauze that shielded him from the truth. And he was happy that when it was all said and done, he would be able to give them the life of their dreams.

"I remember," he said simply.

The siblings smiled at one another and at him. Of course, they could tell he was back before that moment. It was in the way he walked. In the things he spoke about that occurred before the brain operation.

But hearing the words still hit different.

"At the same time because I don't know what I forgot, I'm sure my memories are spotty."

"It's okay, Pops," Spacey said stroking his beard. "Just take your time."

"Yeah, dad, regardless we love you," Minnesota responded, whipping her long black hair over her shoulder.

"I remember holding you as a baby, Minnie. You were so tiny and beautiful."

She grinned.

He turned to Spacey. "I remember flying with you. The trips we would take in my jet when it would be just you and me. I cherish those memories to this day, son."

Spacey's chin rose. "Yep, we stayed up."

He looked at Shay. "I remember helping bring you in this world. I was actually in the room when your mother gave birth too."

"Wow," she smiled, slightly disappointed that he didn't have anything nice to say after the comment. She wanted more.

He looked at Joey and winked.

Where was his memory?

"We must get away. We can't stay in this country. If we do, we will be hunted. So, I have a plan. And I'm asking for your cooperation to see things through."

"You got it, Pops," Joey said disappointed Banks didn't say anything that made him realize he remembered him.

"Whatever you need," Spacey added.

Banks nodded. "Good. Now let's get on with the details so that we can see the promised land."

CHILDREN'S HOME FOR TROUBLED BOYS

The massive home smelled of pine and bleach. Some said it was done to mask the odor of blood and the vile acts that occurred in the night hours, when adults weren't able or interested in saving young souls.

Most rooms were tiny, but Ace's was the largest in the facility. If it weren't for it being in hell it would be considered a suite.

And it was there that Banks sat on the bed with his son, looking into his eyes.

There was great concern in that moment. Because Banks detected an energy brewing in his boy that he wasn't fond of and still he was a Wales.

If he be an animal, Banks was prepared to watch him roar.

As they sat in silence, Ace examined every inch of his young face. You have to understand, he saw his father turn from a beautiful woman into what some would consider, one of the most attractive and powerful men in the world.

Enamored, Ace touched his short cropped curly hair.

Next, he touched the sides of his face, which were dusted with whiskers courtesy of the hormone therapy he participated in to bring him closer to his true identity.

Next the boy's fingertips peddled over the 20-carat earring posted in his ear. The jewel, once caressed, appeared to wink back with a twinkle.

Finally, Ace lifted the medallion on his neck, seduced with so many diamonds it caused his eyes to light up as if dusted with glitter.

The jewelry simply read, WALES.

He released the piece and looked into his father's eyes.

"Will I be like this?" The young man asked.

Banks smiled. "I don't understand."

"When I get older, will I look like you?"

Now he got the beat of his inquiry. "Maybe."

Ace smiled. "Good. Because I like it."

Banks shifted a little.

Hearing Ace say the words almost brought him to his knees. After all, some months back Ace couldn't stand the journey Banks was taking to reclaim his identity. So, witnessing his son saying he wanted to look like him had caused him to flex proudly.

But there were other matters to discuss.

Later for compliments and accolades.

Banks wiped his hands down his thighs. "I heard about the boy, Ace. What's going on?"

The smile on his face wiped away as he walked over to his table. Suddenly he couldn't be bothered with the line of questioning Banks was giving. "Do you want to play?"

Banks rose. "The boy, Ace. Answer me."

Ace sat in his seat. "What about it, father?" He shrugged. "I'm sorry, do you want me to call you father? Or is it still mommy?"

Banks wrinkled his brow, quite aware that the boy was skipping the subject. "I want you to answer my question. Don't make me repeat myself. I'd hate to cave your chest in."

Ace rocked a little, just thinking about the pain. "I didn't mean to make him bleed. If that's what you're asking."

"But you did. And I want to know why."

Ace shrugged. "My other father, Mason, said I can do whatever I wanted when I want because—."

Banks stepped closer. "You have one father. Me. And I explained that to you already. So don't say it again."

"You're right." He pouted and looked down. "I'm just a little boy. I get confused sometimes."

Banks crossed his arms tightly. Ace could fake for the masses, but he knew his son was highly intelligent.

"I'm trying to get you out of here, Ace."

"Why do you want me out? I thought I was here to get better."

"I want you out because you should never have been here in the first place."

"So then get me out."

"I can't if you don't follow the rules." He stepped even closer to his son. His power looming over the child like a 40-year prison sentence. "I can't if you show them that you're...that you're..."

"What is it, father?" Ace grinned.

"I can't help if you keep exhibiting acts of violence."

Ace smiled and looked at the board game in front of him. "They told me that you're really rich. The boys say it's why I got this room."

Silence.

"Are you really rich, father?"

Rich could not touch the wealth that Banks possessed, but he decided to let the young man live with such a small term. "Yes, Ace. I am really rich."

"Then if you're rich, why am I still here?"

Banks sat in the back of his big boy Benz looking at the padfolio again with thoughts of Ace's escape still on his mind. For some reason he felt like he was missing something, and it didn't sit right with his soul.

"Sir," Munro said who was piloting the car.

Banks looked at him.

"The woman you were with last night left her number. Said you can call if you needed a friend."

He smirked and shook his head. "You keep it. I'll let you know if I need it in the future."

Readjusting his shades, he sat deeper into the butter soft leather seats as his thoughts returned on his master plan. Banks wasn't interested in a relationship with any woman.

He only wanted a relationship with his family that consisted of them being safe and forever in peace on their island.

And at the same time, he was still a highly sexual being.

In fact, the more confident he got about his identity, the more he desired a fresh taste of pussy from time to time. But that was the extent of his joy with women.

No one would ever be on his arm for the long term, to hear him tell it, he was done with love.

When he glanced to his right he smiled when he saw two boys playing on the steps of a brownstone. One of the young men had the complexion of a Hershey bar and the other of white chocolate.

The two were tossing a ball back and forth and when the car stopped at a light, they both looked at what they thought was a superstar.

Waving in his direction, Banks eagerly waved back as the boys resumed their activities. They reminded him of he and Mason when they were kids growing up in Baltimore city. So, the smile he held on his face was sincere as his heart thumped with thoughts of the past.

And then he remembered that he didn't fuck with a Lou.

At all.

So, he scowled.

He wanted nothing to do with Mason or anything he represented, especially since he opened his mouth and told Jersey that Banks was responsible for Howard's murder. Which almost got him killed.

Sure, Mason took a bullet for him.

But Banks believed the bullet had his name which is why it caught his spine.

Besides, Lou's were bad news, the city often whispered.

And Banks was just reminded.

But there was something else which also caught his eye on the city street. To the left of the boys stood a man with a crowd around him. Everyone seemed captivated by the hood pastor and Banks was interested in what he had to say.

When the light turned green, he said, "Pull over, Munro. Over there by the crowd. I wanna see something right quick."

"Sure thing, boss."

Once the car was parked, Banks slipped out with Munro standing behind him on guard. Eager and ready to break the back of anyone who stepped his boss's way.

Slowly Banks walked over to the man, who was in his early thirties and wearing a plain white t-shirt, blue jeans, and a pair of grey New Balance sneaks. He wasn't on the flashy side, but his words held a powerful punch.

Even without the pulpit, he was extremely charismatic and looked more like a jewel-less rapper than a man of the cloth.

"...and unless you change the direction of your life you will answer to your past. But I have a secret. You see, some of ya'll don't understand that you can shift. But you must be willing to give up the evil that haunts you. Because most of you are addicted to darkness."

People clapped in agreement.

"See...see...some of you say you want relief. You say you want happiness."

At this point he looked directly at Banks.

Suddenly it was as if they were the only men on the face of the earth.

"But are you willing to give up the repulsive things you love? The violence? The power? The murders?"

Banks shifted, feeling uncomfortable under the man's gaze.

"Because if you don't, karma will visit you, and as sure as I'm standing here, you will lose the thing you love most."

Everyone turned to look at Banks.

Munro wasn't feeling the attention his boss received and so his hand hovered over his waist because at this point it was whatever. Pastor or not, he was ready to make it rain blood.

The preacher had applied pressure and made Banks shutter.

"Man, let's get out of here," Banks walked toward his car, still under the tension of the onlookers.

The pastor never broke stare as they got into the car and drove away.

As Banks walked into one of the office buildings he owned to meet with the head of his security, he couldn't help but think about what the pastor said. The way he appeared to call him out in public had Banks wanting to send one of his people back to teach him respect.

Violently and bloody of course.

But that shit wasn't on the list and so he put his ego in check.

Wearing a black suit, Jan Lopez stood in the middle of the floor with his hands clasped in front of him. Lopez protected some of America's presidents, and as a result knew how to identify and prevent attacks from harming his clients in advance.

And for that Banks paid him well.

The two men shook hands and Banks readjusted his shades. "Put a detail on all of them." He gave him the addresses of his children. "But remember to hang back. If you identify a problem, tell me. I don't want them worried."

"No problem, sir. I have things under control."

CHAPTER TWO

THE UNEASY

The yellow chauffan curtain brushed against Minnesota's face as she stood in front of the open window while pouring two cups of coffee. When she was done, she placed a heavy hand on her belly and smiled.

She couldn't wait to bring new life into the world. A life she was certain she would care about forevermore. After all, she was sure her baby would be the only being she could really love.

Wiping her naturally long black hair out of her face, she walked into her bedroom, placed the cups on the end table and eased back into bed, just as Zercy entered. "Minnie, baby, I told you I was going to get the coffee."

"You were taking too long." She grabbed a cup and sipped. "Who were you talking to anyway? Your sisters?"

He sat on the chair next to the bed. "You're beautiful. Every time I look at you, I thank God that I was able to have a baby with a woman like you."

Her light skin blushed and she sipped again. "Stop it, Zercy." She sat the cup down and pulled her pink robe tighter, so he couldn't see her curves. "You know I hate it when you—."

"I know you don't fuck with compliments. But it's not a compliment if it's the truth." Damn he wanted to taste her pussy.

She pushed a cup across to him. "Drink. Because maybe then you'll stop talking."

"Minnie, I—."

She waved the air. "No, Zercy. Because I thought I made things clear."

"You meant the part when you told me to stay away?" He sat back.

"What else?" She shrugged.

"Well, I can't do that."

She sighed. "Why not?"

"Because you are the mother of my child. My only child. And I can't see not being in your life. I can't see not being able to take care of you. To love you. To taste you. To make love with—"

"You lied."

"I never lied. I—."

She glared. "Don't play fucking games with me!"

Morning tea was over, and she was fully prepared to dig into that ass.

"Don't tell me you only concealed the truth," she continued. "At the end of the day, you didn't tell me Z was your brother!" She slapped one hand into the other. "You didn't tell me you had a twin. I met Z personally and I never liked him. He gives me bad vibes and just knowing you are related to him makes—"

Suddenly he grew heated. "So, is it my fault or yours?" He asked cutting her off.

She glared. "Excuse me?"

"How was I to know your ex-boyfriend had a relationship with my brother?" He placed a hand over his heart. "That's not on me, Minnesota. And you can't charge me with this shit either. The day we met all I saw was you. All I wanted to do was to protect you. Please don't let this come in between us." He dropped his hand by his side. "I don't know what I would do if I lost you."

Minnesota thought about the plans to leave the country with her father and realized that he may have to deal with losing her sooner than later.

When Spacey entered the bedroom, both of them trembled. He wasn't invited and he didn't give a fuck.

"I didn't give you the key to open up the door without knocking, Spacey," Minnesota said adjusting the covers.

"As long as you're in here, I'm getting inside too." He looked at Zercy and back at her. "Now what the fuck is he doing here?" He rubbed his neatly trimmed five o'clock shadow which melted against his vanilla-colored skin.

Spacey had grown into his manhood. He was giving alpha-alpha. Gone were the days of the weakling.

He was more of the evil kind.

"He was just—."

"Get out!" Spacey said, cutting Minnesota off to address her *mans*.

Zercy remained seated while looking at Minnie.

"Now, nigga!" Spacey clapped once.

Annoyed, Zercy stood up and dragged a hand down his face. Walking up to Minnesota he said, "Listen, you don't have to like me right now. But I want you to know that I will do everything in my power to right my wrongs. To do good by you." He touched her belly. "Both of you. And all I'm asking is for a chance."

"Zercy...please don't," she said.

"Minnesota, you are my girl. Whether you realize it now or not. And I love you. All I'm asking is for you not to fall out of love with me."

"This nigga here," Spacey said under his breath.

When he was done Zercy walked out, and she looked at Spacey.

"Before you say anything don't." She walked out of the bedroom and headed to the kitchen with him following.

They both sat down at the table where a basket of fruit sat in the center.

Uneasy with it all, Spacey plopped in the chair. There was so much he wanted to say but he wanted to be tactful too. For a second, his hand rubbed the table before he sat back. "Why was he here, Minnesota? Didn't you say he—."

"You can't do that."

"Do what?"

"Intrude in my relationship."

"Oh, so now it's a problem?"

"You know what I mean."

"Actually, I don't." He paused. "When you said he lied to you and that you felt disrespected, I'm the one you called. And I never refused you. Not once." He pointed at her. "You fucking cried to me. Said you never wanted to see him again. And now all that has changed?"

"I have my reasons. And I know why you don't want me to see him. So don't fake like you're concerned about my health."

"Say what you want, *sis*." He shrugged. "I won't deny my motives. I love you and you know that. But it doesn't mean you can take chances with your life."

"I care about Zercy."

"We often care about the things that are bad for us."

She rose from the table and walked to the refrigerator. As if realizing she didn't want anything out of it, she leaned against the sink. The scent of the fresh fruit sitting in the basket on the island wafted through her nose.

"He's going to betray us! I'm sure."

"Us?" She repeated. "I want my baby to know his father."

"So, what are you going to do?" He chuckled once. "When we leave for the island? Because that kid won't know shit about that nigga then."

She looked down and wiped her hair out of her face again. "I don't know. I haven't thought that far out yet."

"Maybe you should, Minnie. Because at some point you're going to have to let him go. You're going to have to move on. Might as well push off on that shit now."

CHAPTER THREE

BROKEN HUSBAND

Pepper, the nurse, adjusted Mason's shoes as he sat in his wheelchair ready to throw his middle finger up to the world. Paralyzed from the waist down he could no longer do anything by himself. The doctor predicted he would never walk again, and so Mason hated life and every living thing in it.

"Okay, Mrs. Louisville, he's all ready," Adrenna said to Dasher who was sitting on the recliner holding Bolt while looking at TV. "Do you have any questions about his after care?"

Dasher sighed and looked at her husband with irritation. She almost forgot where she was, as Maury stole her focus on television.

But after looking at what she secretly called her "broken husband" she was brought back to reality.

At one point she wanted nothing more than to be Mrs. Mason Louisville. But what was she going to do with *half a man*? She loved the power Mason possessed as he moved around the world. She loved that people feared him and his actions.

But who was going to fear a middle-aged man in a wheelchair?

She didn't see his potential and if truth be told, she hated him for *going and getting himself shot*. All for a man who didn't appreciate him.

When it came to seeing his vision for the future, the woman was blind.

"Mrs. Louisville, do you have any questions on Mason's care?" Adrenna repeated. "Because he will need a lot of assistance."

Dasher blew out a long stream of hot air, looked at the nurse and then Mason. Rolling her eyes, she said, "Nah. If I have a question, I guess I'll call back or whatever." She stomped her foot. "Damn, I don't feel like doing none of this shit! I already got a baby. What I'm gonna do with a big ass man?"

Heartbroken that he chose wrong, Mason looked down at his fingers and sighed.

"Ma'am, that's not fair. You'd be surprised what can happen if you do the exercises the therapists laid out for him. To get his legs stretched and keep the circulation going. Don't listen to these doctors who say he'll never walk again. Give him love and —."

"Are you finished or are you dead?"

Adrenna frowned. "Excuse me? I don't understand the question."

Dasher sat Bolt down and clapped her hand per word. "Are...you...finished...or...are...you...dead?"

"I guess I'm finished but —."

"Good, because the last thing I need is somebody telling me how to raise my husband."

She frowned. "I'm pretty sure he's already grown but whatever, ma'am."

"You know what...these bitches in here be tripping." She scooped up Bolt, stuck him on her hip and attempted to push Mason out of the room with her free hand. But when Adrenna saw she was about to crash him into the wall, she took over the reins.

After he was helped into the backseat of the vehicle by two orderlies, and Bolt was strapped into his car seat, Dasher sped off and drove down the road blasting her music.

Just dumb shit.

She didn't care that Mason was still not well and needed peace and quiet.

She was going to do her regardless and he had better catch up.

It was as if she were a totally different person.

Mason, on the other hand, couldn't believe this was his life and if it wasn't for Bolt reaching and smiling at him in the backseat, he would've preferred to have the car door opened and roll out in the middle of the street as opposed to spending the rest of his life with a woman he wife'd for her beauty and nasty sex game.

When they approached a light, Mason turned to the right and saw two little boys playing on the steps of a brownstone. One of the young men had the complexion of a Hershey bar and the other of white chocolate.

The two were tossing a ball back and forth and when they noticed the stopped car, they both looked at Mason.

Waving in his direction, Mason nodded, and the boys resumed their activities. For some reason, they reminded him of he and Banks when they were kids growing up in Baltimore city.

In that moment he wondered what Banks was doing. He wondered if he hated him for telling Jersey about Howard.

At the same time, where was his own anger?

Where was his rage? It wasn't like Banks didn't kill his son.

But Mason had finally come to terms with one fact.

There was not one single place in his heart, which was capable of hating Banks Wales.

But there was something else which also caught his eye on the city street. To the left of the boys stood a man with a crowd around him. Everyone seemed captivated by the hood pastor and Mason was too.

Rolling down his window he heard the pastor in the grey New Balance say, "...at some point each of us have to answer to the sins of the past. No one is exempt. And if you don't shift your lifestyle and actions, things will get worse. Often visiting your sons. So that they experience the karma you are due."

Mason looked at Bolt who appeared to be okay. Forgetting all about the sons he had lost along the way.

Forgetting about Derrick also.

It wasn't like karma couldn't bite his ass.

"...brace up." The pastor said to the crowd. "You'll need to be strong for this part of the journey."

Without warning, he looked at Mason whose head was damn near hanging out the window due to being captivated by his presence.

"Be strong."

Suddenly everyone looked at Mason who was sitting in the car with his jaw hanging. He was about to ask if he knew him, until Dasher rolled the window up, almost chopping off his nose in the process.

"My air conditioner is on!" She yelled while looking at him through the rear-view mirror. "Shit! Keep my window up! With you broke how I'm gonna pay for gas?"

Mason shook his head at the stupid bitch as they drove away from the scene while the pastor never broke his stare.

The brown Yorkie tore at the bottom of the plastic trash bag until its contents poured out onto the kitchen floor, just as the door opened and Dasher pushed Mason inside in his wheelchair.

"Roof! Roof! Roof! Roof!" The pitter-patter of his paws danced playfully as he saw his master enter.

"Get out the way, boy!" Dasher yelled cheerfully.

Except the dog didn't move out of their path. It took to nipping at Mason's feet as he sat propped in his chair, looking like death. What hurt him the most, was outside of Dasher, not one of his family members came to see him.

Not even the person he wanted most to check on his well-being.

Banks Wales.

Dasher pushed the wheelchair further into the house, propelling Mason so hard he almost crashed into the wall again. She was rough with the chair that's for sure.

And still the dog took to nipping at his feet. If Mason had access to his legs, he would have kicked the animal across the room. Instead, he was forced to observe the animal gnawing at his big toe, while trying to understand why he couldn't feel pain.

"Get out the way, Lockman!"

When the animal didn't move, she picked him up and hurled him across the room.

"Why you do that shit?" He yelled seeing the abuse.

She waved the air. "He'll be fine."

What the fuck? He thought.

"I do that all the time. Now, are you hungry?" Dasher said excitedly as Bolt sat on the side of her hip like a gun on a belt.

He shook his head nah.

She rolled her eyes. "Mason, how much longer are you going to be fucking sad? So, what you got shot. So, what you can't walk. You'll get over it. At least you got me. I mean, ain't that good enough?"

Not really.

He looked up at her and glared. "Are you serious? My life is changed, Dasher! Of course I'm still fucked up."

"Wow, you can talk," she said sarcastically.

She propped Bolt into a car seat that sat on the sofa and shoved Mason into the living room. It was almost as if she was trying to see how far she could launch him around.

"I was shot. I didn't break a leg, Dasher."

"And again, I get all that. But shouldn't you be happy you made me your wife in time to take care of you? I mean really."

He looked down. "Dasher, I get that I should be grateful, but you don't know what I'm—."

"Why are you telling me things I already know? I was the one speaking with your doctors. I was the one checking to be sure you had your medicine. Me!" She stabbed herself into the center of the chest with a stiff finger. "And you over here talking like you don't owe me nothing."

He looked up at her and then downward.

She was right in a lot of ways.

Dasher had proven to be stand up during his recent turn of events. But she was also an annoying woman. Always standing over him and lurking. Still, he was at times grateful to have her in his life. After all, it beat being alone.

At least that's what he told himself.

"Mason, you have to cheer up, baby. You will be happy you chose me." She rubbed him between the legs which did nothing but make his dick itch. "Trust me. I know it doesn't feel that way now but it's definitely true."

He sighed. "Maybe."

"Maybe?" She frowned and squeezed his balls. There was a smile on her face, but it was obvious she was trying to hurt him.

"Let me go." He said slowly, despite the pain.

She didn't.

"Now."

She released him. "I was just playing, silly."

He stroked the pain off his dick. "Where is my phone, Dasher?"

She glared and dusted dried baby spit off her cheek. "I'll get it to you in a second. Don't rush me."

"You said that the last six times I asked."

"Why do you want it so badly? Let's talk about that shit." She clapped several times.

"I want to find out why my son hasn't been by. I mean, have they come to see me? Has anybody come?"

"You mean like your precious Banks?"

"Has he, Dasher? Has anybody?"

"Spend time with me," she smiled. "Trust me, you'll have plenty of time to get up with Banks and the rest of your little ass crew. At the end of the day, you must remember that you're married now." She walked closer. "But if you forget, don't worry. I'll help remind you."

"I haven't spoken to my son. And every time I try to talk to him, you find a reason to throw me off."

"Mason, you were in intensive care. You weren't doing well. And as your wife, it was my duty to ensure that nothing stood in the way of your health. As a matter of fact, you look like you hurting. Let me get you together right quick."

She kissed him on the cheek, dug in the baby's diaper bag and removed a pill bottle. Releasing a few from captivity, she grabbed some water and walked over to him.

Shaking the pills in the center of her palm like dice she said, "Open wide."

He started to fight; besides he was done with alcohol and drugs. But he was in amazing pain and welcomed some relief. "You know you want them, Mason. Don't

fake." She giggled. "Trust me, you won't get addicted.
I'll never let that happen."

"When I wake up, I need to talk to my son. No more
excuses. I have to let him know that I'm okay."

"Mason, I got you." She winked.

"I'm serious!"

"Open wide, nigga," she said firmer.

He swallowed the pills. No liquid.

"That's my man." She grinned.

CHAPTER FOUR

THE SMELL OF IRON

The day started off slow for the oldest Lou son and he was hoping things would change.

After doing a few laps, Derrick slid out of the heated pool inside the Louisville Estate when he heard his phone ring.

Expecting a call from his mother, Jersey, who he hadn't heard from since she shot Mason accidently, he was worried that something might have happened to her.

Apart from his son Patrick and his brothers Bolt, Ace, and Walid, as it stood, it seemed as if the Louisville brand was doomed to perish. It was as if their fate was to live and then die young and he didn't understand why.

What had they done so wrong outside of everything?

And then there was his father who he hadn't spoken to at all. Every time he went to see about him in the hospital his actions were blocked. And since Dasher was his wife, there wasn't much he could do except beg for details which she provided sparingly.

Yes, something felt off with his new stepmother Dasher Louisville. That was certain.

And he was determined to find out what.

Derrick heard somewhere in his travels that you should always pick a partner who loved you more than you loved them. That you should select a person that cared so much about you, that they would do all they could to make the relationship work.

But now he was starting to believe they were wrong.

Dasher wanted Mason Louisville more than anything, and the way she acted back in the day when no one was looking, he felt she wanted his father more than she wanted baby Bolt.

When Derrick's dick jumped, he realized he hadn't fucked Shay in months. It wasn't like the man didn't try. He did everything to get her in the mood, but she was stopping all his actions.

She even blocked him from her social media accounts and when he asked why she stared at him like she didn't understand the English language. The man had plans to play along for a little while, because when it came to Shay, he definitely wanted the woman in his life. But his dick would be in something moist before the end of the week, period.

After drying off from the pool, he answered the ringing cell. Looking at the caller he shook his head. "What you want, man? I said I would hit you back." He wiped the water droplets off his belly.

"Nigga, fuck all that bullshit you spitting. You coming to the spot tonight or what?"

"Nah." He dried the dampness from under one arm with the towel.

"Why not?"

"I told you my wife been suspect."

"Fuck you do?"

"Like you give a fuck." He sat in the chair and rubbed his chest.

"All I'm saying is that we got the bitches, zips, edibles and —."

"Derrick, can we talk?"

He turned around to see Shay standing behind him. Even though there was sadness in her eyes, he couldn't get over how gorgeous she was. She was wearing red shorts and a white t-shirt with no bra. And because she went to the salon her painted toes were the color of undriven snow.

"I'm on the phone." He turned back around and tossed the towel on the floor. "Uh, like I was saying. I'm not going to be able to —."

"Derrick!" Shay said louder.

The Louisville heir was annoyed. "Listen, let me hit you back." He ended the call and dropped his cell on the pool chair to his right. "What?"

"We need to talk."

"Oh, so now you wanna rap? Because when I came to you about not knowing what was happening with my mother or father, you ain't have no conversation for me. But had it been Banks you would've given your life for—."

"I *know*, Derrick."

He glared. *Damn she was annoying.* "You know about what?"

"About Flower."

He shuffled his feet out in front of him as if he were trying to put a motorcycle in gear. And his dick shriveled up a bit upon hearing the news.

Now he knew what was wrong with her over the weeks.

"Uh, what, I mean, you, are we going to, uh, is what about her?"

She shook her head. "You know, I loved you for a long time, Derrick. As a matter of fact, I didn't even love Harris as much as I cared about you."

"Shay, go 'head with that bullshit. Why the fuck is it always something with you? Why can't we just chill and be with one another? How come—."

"I have wanted you from the moment we decided that it would be just me and you against the world. And at first, I didn't know why I was so obsessed."

"Fuck, man! Ain't nobody trying to hear all this shit."

Derrick was on some mad ignorant game, but guilt had a way of making a nigga lose reason.

"I never knew when I gave you my heart that you would be responsible for one of the most painful moments in my life, only second to finding out that Harris was dead." She shook her head. "I felt like I deserved more when you hurt me. But I finally realized why I felt like you were perfect for me."

He flopped back. "Okay, I'm listening."

"Because you a Lou. You trash. And I felt that trash was all I deserved. I felt like it was impossible to get better."

"You out here calling Lou's trash?"

"It's true!"

"Shay for the millionth time I'm not cheating on you!"

"But you are though." She paused. "I didn't tell you about the pics or videos I found in your phone because your father had been shot. And you didn't know where Jersey was." She laughed once. "But I'm sick of waiting for you to see the pain in my eyes. I'm sick of waiting for you to acknowledge that something is wrong with me. I'm sick of waiting on you to give a fuck."

"First of all, I ain't fuck nobody but—."

"Don't lie, Derrick. I'm warning you. Say you didn't fuck her again and I won't be held liable for what I do next."

"Are you threatening me?"

"I said what I said. And I'm sick of the lies popping out of your mouth."

"I'm not lying." He rose and walked toward the door. "And I'm not about to listen to this ignorant ass conversation either. But if you want to put on like the victim, then that's on you. Just don't ask me to stick around while you do it. I'm going out tonight."

"But you not though." She said following him from behind.

When he turned around, she whacked him in the head with a steel *Louisville* slugger bat.

The irony of it all.

The basement was almost black…

Derrick woke up on the floor with Shay sitting across from him in a metal chair. There was a small window in the upper wall that allowed the moonlight to shine inside. Other than that, all that could be seen were shadows.

Derrick rubbed his temples and tried to sooth a headache so throbbing he could hardly lift his head.

"How did you get me down here?" He asked dragging himself toward the wall, so that his back lie against it.

She was now wearing red panties and a white tank top and next to her was the silver Louisville bat that she used to hit him with earlier.

It was still coated with his blood.

"What's going on, baby?" Derrick asked. "Why would you…why would you do that to me?"

"Do you love me?" She whispered.

"You know what, despite what you did, I do love you." He touched his head. "But I also know if you don't get me help, I'll be in trouble. I could die, Shay. Is that what you want?"

She rose, and he caught a glimpse of her nipples hardening under her shirt. "Is the dick mine too?" She said seductively.

As she asked the question, he couldn't get over how much she looked like a mad woman. He didn't see his loving spouse anymore.

He saw a stranger.

"You know this dick is yours," he said, gripping it something like the way he used to, despite his wrist being a little limp on the tug.

"Will you get hard for another woman?" She rose her foot and gently peddled his dick with her toes.

"What? No!" He proclaimed. "I'm done with these stupid ass hoes out here! I promise."

Shay smiled and walked over to the door. Within seconds, two women appeared. One white. The other black.

They were wearing bodycon short dresses and they smelled of unwashed men.

"Shay, what is this?" He asked looking up at her.

"Well, I know you love whores. And since you love whores, I figure what better way to show you how much I care, than giving you what you desire."

"So, you think I'm gonna fuck these bitches? In front of you. Like I didn't put a ring on your finger. Come on, Shay. You know me better than that."

The white girl slithered to his left, the black to his right. Within seconds they were kissing him on his ear. Even tasting the dried blood that ran down on the sides of his face moments earlier.

Before long, his dick was standing tall for the pledge of Hoe-Liegence.

Shay shook her head. "I'm standing right across from you and still you respond to another woman."

The white girl grabbed his dick and when it was thick and throbbing, she eased on top of it. She smelled of wet dough and iron.

What shocked Derrick was that she was already wet. It took him a few seconds to realize she was on her period, and bleeding all over his dick.

But why couldn't he get soft?

Shay would never believe him now.

Up and down, she rose until he was so hard, he was pulsating.

Looking at his wife across the room, who had tears in her eyes, all he could do was shake his head. Had she fucked him he probably would not have gotten hard.

"I'm so sorry," he mouthed. "I'm sorry."

With that he grabbed the stranger's waist and bust inside her pinkness.

WALID

Walid stood in front of his mirror after dropping his white t-shirt over his head. Since Ace had been gone, he spent a huge amount of time staring at himself in the mirror which confused Morgan and the nanny who came on the weekends.

Some said his actions were due to vanity. But Banks knew the truth. Walid wasn't being vain. He was doing all he could to see his brother's face which was an exact replica of his own.

He missed him that much.

When Walid's bedroom door opened and Banks walked inside, Walid approached him. "Is it today?"

"No, son."

He looked down. His little world rocked to the core. "Then when?"

Banks walked deeper into the prince's room and flopped on the bed. Next, he softly grabbed Walid's hand, tugging him closer.

"I know you're upset. But it's going to take time. I just want you to realize that I'm doing everything I can to—"

"Why is it taking so long?" He glared, as he softly pulled his hand away.

"Because Ace made some mistakes. Mistakes he was too young to understand had repercussions at the time."

Walid trembled a little. "But...but he..."

"Listen, Walid, Ace will be okay, but we will have to wait a bit longer to bring him home. But I want you to trust me when I say, he will come back."

Walid stared at him for a second and walked away. Flopping into his burgundy leather game chair, he was preparing to play a round on his Play Station 5. "Whatever you say."

"Son."

"Yes?"

"We were still talking."

"I know."

"So why did you walk away?"

"Because I want my brother back. If I can't get him back, maybe I'll have to be bad too. Then we can be together."

CHAPTER FIVE

THE LIVING DEAD

VIRGINIA BEACH, VIRGINIA

I t started to rain as Jersey rolled out of bed and planted her feet into the thin beige carpet in the hotel room, she was posted up inside. The moment she opened her eyes and remembered her crimes, she released a soft sigh.

Every day ran into the other and she was looking for an end to it all. The woman was bored. So much so, that she masturbated many times the night before. To the point of the seat of her panties being slick, gooey and uncomfortable.

She didn't touch herself to reach an orgasm. That was the least of her concerns. She did it to sleep. Because ever since she shot her ex-husband, the father of her children, guilt whispered evil things to her in the thick of the night.

Things she would have taken to heart if she didn't have hope.

Hope of forgiveness.

Hope of love.

And still she realized returning to the way things used to be was just wishful thinking. After all, without knowing it at the time, the moment she pulled the trigger she made a move that would forever change her life.

Banks could no longer trust her.

Walking to the window, she opened the curtains overlooking the beach. Not many people were outside, due to the rain, and so the sand was dampened with heavy droplets.

But now it was time.

Time to do what she wasn't built for in the moment.

Time to do what she feared.

Picking up her cell she made a phone call. It felt like forever but when she heard his voice her knees buckled. It had been so long. "Hey...hey, Banks."

"How are you?" Banks asked calmly.

She smiled.

That voice was like melted butter on warm toast, and she reasoned by his tone that maybe he still cared. "I'm fine," she sighed. "I mean, all things considered. I could be doing much better, but I won't complain."

"That's good, Jersey."

The way he said her name was so fucking sexy.

"Banks, I...."

"You don't have to say anything."

"I do." She inhaled and exhaled. "I have to, and I would've done it sooner if I thought you would want to hear from me." She looked down at her feet and back at the sea. "I...I mean, I'm sorry for, for you know..."

"Trying to kill me?"

His words knocked her into the chair next to the window. "Yes. Banks, I'm so fucking sorry. I acted without thinking and now I've ruined everything."

"Don't worry."

"When I heard about Howard's death, and you possibly killing him from Mason, I made a mistake. I snapped."

"Snapped huh?"

"Yes, and all I want to do is get back to us. Back to where we left off. All I want is for things to be as they were, Banks. Because I...I know you would never hurt my son. And I let Mason get into my head, like he always does."

Silence.

"Um, we have to be stronger," she continued when he sounded like he was tapping out. "When all we ever wanted was to be together. You never would've hurt my son. I know that now."

"I killed him."

She rose.

Her eyes widened.

"What...what did you just say?"

"I had him murdered for what he did to Bet. And now I'm learning he also raped Spacey. So, hear me when I tell you this, I did the world a favor by getting rid of that nigga. And I know you know that."

She walked over to the bed and flopped down, almost missing it by inches. "Banks, I...I don't know what to say."

"So, you were right to aim at me with that gun. But you were wrong to miss, Jersey."

"Banks, I...I don't understand. Why would you hurt me like this? I know we had our problems but the way you're telling me you killed him is...cold."

Her mind was all over the place. On one end she wanted revenge for her son and on the other she knew what kind of man the boy she'd given birth to was.

He was evil.

TRUCE 4: THE FINALE   73

He was selfish.

But he was a Lou.

She also knew what kind of man Banks was. He was a real-life king, with the money and power capable to make all her dreams come true. Did she really want to give it all up for the ghost of her son's memories?

To toast to his cold bones?

She shook her head slowly to get rid of the idea of what may have happened to Howard. "Is...is Mason okay?"

"I don't know, Jersey. And I don't give a fuck. My focus has been clear these days. All I want is my son back."

She nodded. "You are the first person I called since I ran. I haven't even spoken to Derrick because I'm afraid the phone is tapped. I only spoke to you and Carrie to be sure Blakeslee is okay. Although she hasn't been answering the phone either. That's another reason why I wanted to —."

"She's with me."

"But she—."

"Blakeslee is my flesh and blood, Jersey. And I'm not about to let a sitter or anybody else for that matter, stop me from getting everybody out."

"Out of where?"

"You know."

"So, you're still leaving? Without me?"

"My plans didn't change just because you missed your shot." He paused. "I can't believe you ran and left my little girl with a stranger."

She placed a hand over her heart. "But the nanny's very experienced. I never would have left her with—."

"Jersey, don't concern yourself with my daughter, or my family from here on out. All the energy you have should be focused on yourself."

"Your family? But what about me?"

Silence.

"Banks, please, I want to come home. If you still leaving, why can't I go with you? I'm the one who helped you work out the details. I'm the one who helped you pick out every design on that island. Even the mansion on the property was my idea. I mean, since I'm wanted by the police, don't I deserve to live in paradise too?"

"Let me be clearer, I can't fuck with you no more."

"Banks, I'm dead without you. I won't make it! Please don't do this."

"Take care. The police are still looking for you. For what you did to Mason and the two police officers you supposedly murdered some time back in the day. Before Skull Island. But judging by what you said I guess you know that already."

"I won't let you walk away from me!"

"You don't control what happens. I do."

"Banks, if you do this you will regret it! I will not be abandoned. I will not be treated like some side bitch!"

"It's not up for discussion. Don't call me again, Jersey. I'm giving you instructions on what it takes to live out the rest of your life. Heed my warning."

CHAPTER SIX

OUTMATCHED

Ziggy, Zuri and Ziamond were sitting in Ziamond's truck on the way home. All three looked as if they had been in a fight because, well, they had been in a fight. The siblings were bullies. Always looking for trouble. And so, they got their hearts' desire.

All three had blood drops in their wild curly hair.

Their lips were swollen.

Their flesh was bruised.

And Ziggy and Zuri had loose teeth.

Had they stayed in their own lanes and minded their own business, it could've all been so simple.

But nothing ever was easy for the triplets.

All of the drama, every ounce, was due to their inability to know their places and remain in their own lanes. The women craved adventure, even if it meant playing with their very lives.

Last week they discovered that Ziamond's boyfriend had plans to move out of the apartment they shared together for over a year. She thought things were going fine in their relationship. She thought they were the perfect couple.

She thought wrong.

Ziamond was an abusive girlfriend in every sense of the word. The man couldn't have a life. She managed the time he spent out of their home. Checked the odometer to be sure the miles added up to the places he said he'd been. She even had codes to his phones, computers, and banking accounts.

Ziamond was a bitter, nasty woman.

She was vile.

She was angry.

And she was in emotional pain.

She ruled her relationships with an iron fist and her sisters were her sergeants in arms. If someone were to take Ziamond as their woman, they had better be ready for the lot of them. It didn't help matters that the other two were single and so in their free time they followed George around as their sister wished.

No longer able to control Zercy, they eagerly looked for another victim. And unfortunately for George, he was it. They took joy reporting back to their sister the findings which were uneventful.

They found no evidence that the man was cheating. He seemed innocent.

And then the moving truck arrived in front of the apartment. The two sisters were on glue as they watched Ziamond's man leave, under the cover of night when Ziamond was taking care of business for Zantonio.

And he was quick too.

Moving so fast they couldn't tell their sister in time what was happening because she didn't answer the phone.

So, they took matters in their own hands.

From afar they followed the truck to its next destination which ended up being a cottage style home where a beautiful chocolate girl welcomed him with open arms and two grey French bulldogs.

They left without drama that night.

Before George knew it the triplets returned with Ziamond who was livid that once again, a man had decided he didn't want to be in her life. The thing was George's new girl wanted all the smoke with the Triplets.

In the end her brothers and cousins beat the curls out of their heads and Ziamond decided that she would let things go for the moment.

She had no choice.

They were outmatched.

But the thirst for revenge still lingered. Like a crazed dog who had its first taste of human blood. They wanted someone to pay.

They cared not about the guilt or innocence of their next victim.

After the melee was over, and they pulled up to Ziamond's house they were surprised to see Zercy's car out front.

"What is he doing here?" Ziamond said touching her swollen lip.

"Fuck if I know." Zuri responded. "Let's go find out."

When they walked inside, they were shocked to see Zercy sitting in the living room, on the sofa. His forearms were atop his thighs and his hands were clutched together in anger.

"I'm happy to see you, big brother," Ziamond said. "But...but what are you doing here?"

"What did you want that you called me so much for today, Zuri?"

She cleared her throat. "Um...it was about Ziamond's boyfriend."

"It's always about something with ya'll. Every fucking day!"

"Wait, why you mad at us?" Zuri asked.

"Let me make it simple. Since the three of you have intruded in my personal life, I have lost everything new. Everything I love."

"Brother, are you good? 'Cause you acting real offensive." Ziamond asked, touching her bruised lip again. It throbbed, that part was true. But she was mainly doing it to solicit sympathy. It didn't work. "Because we may need you. My ex-boyfriend —."

"I don't give a fuck what you need!"

The triplets looked at one another.

"What I *need* is for you three bitches to stay out of my life. From here on out. No coming by. No asking

questions. No calls. Do I make my fucking self-clear?"
He yelled louder, standing up.

Silence.

It had to be silent.

You must understand, Zercy was a spiritual man.
He was tapped into the God energy that built worlds.
The problem was, where two or more agree there was
power.

And the triplets were a threesome.

That meant he had three people, four if you included
their brother Zantonio, who were dead set on ruining
his life to keep their family secrets intact.

"You really don't give a fuck about us no more, do
you?" Zuri asked.

"I can't even begin to tell you what I think right
now."

Ziamond shook her head. "We just walked in here
beat down and bloodied. And you coming at us about

that bitch who out in the world fucking her own brother?" Ziamond asked.

He stepped closer.

They trembled.

He walked in front of them.

"Stay out of my life." He looked at all three of them directly in the eyes. "This is my last warning. You don't know the things I'm capable of. But I do." He stomped toward the door, knocking them over in the process.

Z stood in front of his sisters who were so angry they were shivering about what they deemed as disrespect from their brother.

There were very few times in life where Z got upset.

The first came when he lost his pussy business due to the police asking questions about his friend Myrio, who he believed Minnesota was responsible for killing.

Law enforcement snooped around so much, that before long he had to get out of the pussy business.

The second time came when he learned that once again, his brother appeared to choose a woman over family.

What was it about these females that made him so vulnerable to their feminine wiles?

Needing to console his sister, he walked up to them and embraced them into a big hug. Wiping the tears from each of their faces he said, "Don't worry. I'll find out how to strike this bitch. Give me a couple of days."

"I heard one of his twins is in the troubled boys home and Banks wants to get him out." Ziamond said. "Maybe we should take a trip."

"We can do that later. I have a few ideas of my own," Zantonio said.

"Are you sure you can do this?" Zuri said.

"I got it. Trust." He kissed her on the cheek and got down to business.

Except, Z didn't allow a few days to pass.

He remembered a while back that he heard Banks often saw a doctor in Baltimore county for his hormone therapy. And so, he staked out the facility he visited.

That's all he needed.

Within a few hours, Banks came, and he had him right where he wanted.

From a far, Z followed the man to the hanger where he talked to a pilot. Next to an upscale luggage spot where Banks exited with an expensive suitcase set. He even trailed him to several small businesses he owned, which he was liquidating in preparation for the flight.

Instead of following him further, he decided to walk into the sandwich shop Banks visited last after he left.

The moment Z entered the establishment, the first thing he noticed was how clean and neat everything was. Even the meat in the cooler appeared to be vibrant as if it were painted.

Easing to the counter, he was approached by an older white man with kind blue eyes. "How can I help you son?"

"Um, I like this place." Z nodded looking around.

"Why thank you."

"If you ever interested in selling, I'll buy."

The man smiled wider. "Unfortunately, that won't happen."

He frowned. "Why is that?"

"Because I was gifted it back just now. And I plan to leave it for my daughter. So, she can learn the importance of ownership."

"Gifted?" Z repeated.

"Yep. My boss is leaving the country. And out of the blue, he gave me the business that was started when I was a little boy back to me."

"I get it." Zantonio grinned and walked toward the door.

"Did you want a sandwich?"

"Nah, shawty, I'm full." He walked out.

An hour later he called some of the most unsavory killers and gutter trash ever to walk Baltimore city. Having a plan for revenge, he extended an invitation to these men to his house. Most didn't know Z's purpose, but they knew if an invite was offered to his lavish estate, then he meant business.

As the men stood in the dining room, Z approached them. "I called you all here because I need your help. And afterwards, I'm one hundred percent confident that this information will make you some of the wealthiest men in Maryland."

"What that mean?" Shopper asked. He was a tall black man with one regular eye and the other covered by a material that looked like a piece of white silk.

"The Wales' are leaving the country. And I guarantee, that if you can grab one of them, just one, the price to free them will be heavy. I'm talking millions."

The men looked at one another and rubbed their calloused hands together.

"To make it even sweeter, I'll personally add one hundred thousand for anybody who will bring me Minnesota Wales. Alive is good. Raped, beaten and bloodied is even better."

They cheered and a few even grabbed their dicks.

"By the way, the kids are worth fifty grand each." He smiled.

"How much for Banks?" Shopper yelled.

"Get him, and I know a few people who will pay $500,000."

More cheers.

"Do what you do best, outlaws. But bring them to me ASAP. Time is of the essence."

CHAPTER SEVEN

THE WEIRDEST SPIN

River stood in front of the window in her apartment overlooking Baltimore. The smell of bacon wafted through her nose and caused her belly to rumble. She hadn't eaten in days, due to worry. So, she was happy that at least her appetite had returned.

"It's ready!"

She turned around and smiled at Tinsley who was wearing a silk pink robe with strawberries speckled throughout.

"I hope you love it. I made the bacon exactly the way you like. Crisp, close to burnt but not really."

River flopped on the sofa and pushed aside a comforter and pillow where he slept the night before since his old room now held River's workout equipment. "Thanks. I'm definitely starved."

Tinsley handed her a bacon and egg sandwich on a plate decorated with cantaloupe. He made the meal a presentation.

Eager to get her opinion, he sat across from her and waited for her first bite, hoping desperately that she would enjoy the meal.

She ate.

He grinned. "Well?"

"It's good." She nodded. "But you know that shit already, don't you? You never had a problem in the kitchen."

He chuckled and grew serious. "Thank you for letting me stay, River. Like, I really love being around you."

"You have plenty places to go." She wiped the corners of her mouth and continued to chew. "Banks been said you could move in when you're ready."

"I know, but I want to be here."

She sat her plate down on the table, dusted her hands, and sat back deeper into the sofa. "What's on your mind, Tin?"

He pulled his robe closed. "Nothing."

"Tin…"

He looked down and back at her. "You. You are on my mind."

She frowned. "In what way?"

"After we did what we did at the hotel…it's like—"

"What we do exactly?" She interrupted. "Because if you ask me, ain't shit went down that need to be talked about in the daytime."

"I know that."

"Then why I gotta keep saying it every couple of days?"

"River, we—."

"Tin, I'm gay!"

"So am I."

"You know what I fucking mean! I'm into women. Being with you in that way puts the weirdest spin on a heterosexual relationship I ever seen. And I'm not into making statements to prove we can be together by changing what I like."

"What you like? Why do we have to fit into boxes? We're bigger than that, River. If you love me and I love—."

"I like pussy. That's it. And you wearing a wig ain't gonna make me forget that shit."

Tinsley felt like he had been dropped down an elevator shaft. "But you wanted me when we were in that hotel room. You responded to me then, didn't you? The way you breathed and moved into me was more passionate than any man I ever fucking been with. Why won't you accept that?"

"We will never be together in that way again. Do you hear me?" She grabbed the rest of her sandwich and stormed away.

BANKS

The office was too small and yet they were having a very important meeting in the Children's Home for Troubled Boys.

"Mr. Wales, I understand what you want." Dr. Hughes said clasping her hands together. "You've made yourself clear." She leaned back in her seat and the top of it bumped against the wall due to not having enough room. "But Ace is exhibiting some more behavior that is concerning."

Banks shifted. "This place is overwhelmed. You shouldn't be handling children who have mental issues and children who made one-time mistakes like Ace."

"I can assure you Ace is in the right place."

His jaw twitched and he looked up at the ceiling. Lately light gave him the worst headache. Removing his shades from the front of his shirt and placing them on he said, "Listen, I know he hurt the boy."

"Correction. He stabbed the boy."

"I get that and—."

"He actually got involved in another child's business, Mr. Wales. So, I don't think you really get what's happening here. He took it upon himself to stab a child with a fork and threatened to do it again later."

Banks crossed his legs, ankle to knee. "From what Ace told me the one kid was touching people inappropriately at night." He threw his hands up in the air. "His words not mine. So maybe you need to check that situation out instead of blaming Ace. Because I told him to drop anybody violating him in that way."

"And again, that accusation was unfounded. Even if it were true, that wasn't Ace's responsibility to correct. As a result, we have to keep him longer to investigate what is causing these violent outbreaks. It's not just for Ace's own good. But it's for you too. Because the last thing you need is that child growing up to be a man who will inevitably end up harming you."

Banks' jaw twitched. "How much longer does he have to stay here?"

"As long as it takes."

"Nah." He shook his head slowly. "It won't be that long." He leaned to the left. "That's the bottom line."

She caught his drift but decided not to push the issue in that moment. "There's another matter."

"There always is with you people."

"Your butler. In prison."

"What about him?" He shrugged.

"He killed someone in your home. And it was said that he may have other information about atrocities that the twins could have witnessed. Maybe —."

"My butler hung himself in a jail cell last night." He said through clenched teeth. "And if you ask me, he did that because they kept trying to pressure him to admit to things he didn't witness. Yes, he murdered my aunt due to what she did to Ace. By giving him the bow and arrow. But we weren't involved in any crimes and he said that to the authorities repeatedly before he took his own life. But they didn't believe him. His blood is on their hands."

"Well, what about Jersey Louisville?"

"What about her?" He shrugged.

"Until she's found, we still don't feel comfortable releasing him to you. We don't even feel comfortable with Walid being in your—."

"What does her going missing have to do with anything?"

"Well let's look at the entire design. Outside of your butler kidnapping, raping and murdering a woman in your house and Jersey shooting Mason in your home, along with your older children being held captive in an attic for years, I think it's more than enough reason for us to be at least skeptical. The question we should be asking is if Walid is safe with you?"

Banks was appalled with how much she knew. "You won't take another one of my sons." The comment was heavy and laced with threats. "I promise you that."

"Sir, please don't threaten me."

"It's not a threat. Ace doesn't belong here. And I'm giving you less than a week to come to your senses."

"Look, I'm not the person who makes the final decision."

He glared. "You didn't tell me that before."

"It's true."

"Well, who handles releasing my boy? Why the fuck am I talking to you?"

Silence.

"Who handles it?!" He yelled.

"Her name is Dr. Marjorie Holman."

"Where is she now?"

"She is with her boyfriend. Well, he's kind of her boyfriend but he isn't really ready to commit."

He stepped closer to the desk. It's funny how she was tight lipped before because she was an old chatty bitch now. "If I discover you're lying, I will be back." He got up and walked away.

Banks walked out of the doctor's office while talking on the phone. To his left was Munro who was actively guarding his person, but that wouldn't stop the slime sitting in a black pickup truck in the parking lot from getting excited.

"There he go right there," Organ said groping his dick before looking back at his friend.

"Should we snatch him now?" Koran asked.

"Fuck yeah! Once he get back to the house it'll be too late."

Eager to get that paper, both eased out the car, with guns tucked in their waists. They were within ten feet of their victims and their mouths were watering. Just thinking about bagging a billionaire had him horny.

Suddenly Organ was snatched away.

When Koran looked behind, he was confused.

"Where you at, nigga?" He whispered retracing his steps.

When he bent the corner, where an alley met the buildings, he was shocked to see his friend lying on the ground, marinating in his own blood.

Turning around to run, he was met with a bullet to the forehead for his efforts.

Just that quickly Banks' security prevented an attack, all without him knowing.

CHAPTER EIGHT

BITE MY THIGHS

The ambiance was romantic, but it wasn't about business as River sat at the bar with Jock one of Mason's men. They were such regulars that the bartender left the whiskey bottle on top despite it being against the law.

But big money had its own set of rules.

Everyone knew that.

"...I still think you're overreacting, River." He grabbed a fry, popped it in his mouth and soaked it with his drink. "Maybe you should relax."

"This why I can't stand dealing with dumb niggas sometimes." She shook her head. "I know something's wrong, and not one of ya'll niggas give a fuck. Which is foul considering how much he does for you."

"I'm dumb because I refuse to think his wife may be fucking with him?" He chuckled once. "Maybe you should stay outta nigga business and — ."

"I never said she was hurting him, Jock. What I said was that she's not letting me talk to him. And to me that's suspicious, especially since she knows the type of relationship we have."

"What about Derrick?" He sipped his whiskey.

"What about him?"

He chuckled again which she found profoundly annoying. "Is he saying anything about his father?"

She took a sip. "Actually, I haven't heard from him in over a week. Which is another reason I feel like something's off."

"Did you talk to him on a regular before?"

She wiped her mouth with the back of her hand. "Nah. Me and Derrick didn't have much of a — "

"Do you even have a relationship with Dasher?"

"Not really. At first, Mason treated her crib like a trap. She basically went from holding product at her spot to being his baby mother then wife. So, I still don't know what the fuck is going on. For all I know she did something to Derrick too. And maybe even Bolt."

He shook his head, drowned everything in his glass and poured another. "So let me get this straight. First you think his wife may be doing something to him. Then you think she may be doing something to his sons? And you want me to step to the boss's wife with that weak ass case?"

"Look, I'm—."

"Nah, until you got proof, I say stay the fuck out the way. Or you could make shit bad with Mason when he gets better. He may even turn his gun on you."

MASON

Although he had a throbbing headache, Mason finally opened his eyes and was temporarily blinded by the brightness. The window was ajar, and the curtains flapped hypnotically in the breeze.

Looking to his left he noticed his wife was not in bed.

Pulling his wheelchair closer, he used his upper body to slam his lower body in place. Damn, at one point he could go and do whatever he desired. And now he was dependent on the mercy of others.

For a second, he froze in place and looked out the window as he took in the view. It wasn't a Louisville or Wales mansion, but the property did have a little personality.

What he wouldn't give to go back to the past. Even if it meant going back to his childhood when he had zero control over the situations in and around his life. But there was no use in wishful thinking.

Hands firmly on the wheels, he rolled into the living room and then the kitchen, where he saw Dasher scrambling eggs with nothing but a pink thong and bra. Beautifully crisp bacon and fresh omelets with seafood lay before him but he didn't have much of an appetite.

"Smells good," he said more to spark conversation than anything else. "I appreciate you cooking."

"Hey you!" Dasher said, turning around to look at him before focusing back on the stove.

Mason rolled toward Bolt who was sitting in a highchair at the table. Loving how perfect the child was, he playfully squeezed his little foot. The baby cooed and offered a gummy grin.

Looking at Dasher he said, "Where's my phone? Gotta make a few calls."

"So, are you hungry? Because I've been trying to get you to eat something for days."

He glared. "Dasher, where is my cell?"

With her back toward him she continued to cook. Except now the utensils slammed inside the pan. "Stop worrying about your fucking phone! It's not going anywhere! Focus on your family for once in your life so—."

"I want my fucking phone, bitch! Now!" He rolled closer, almost kissing the back of them ankles with his wheels.

"You know…" her voice deepened. "I'm so sick of you not appreciating me around here."

He frowned and rolled back an inch.

"You don't know what I went through when you were shot, Mason. You don't know the mental damage it put on me. When are you going to start asking me how I feel around this bitch? Asking me what I want? Huh?" Slowly she turned around and faced him.

Mason didn't understand what Man Voice wanted but he had zero sympathy for her in that moment.

"I need to call my son. I need to tell him I'm okay. And I need my phone, Dasher. Don't fuck with me or—."

"Or what? Just what the fuck do you plan to do from down there? Bite my thighs, nigga? Huh? You don't scare nobody no more!"

She removed the hot pan off the stove.

"What...what you doing?" He asked rolling away.

She moved closer.

He rolled back faster.

But she was quicker and before he could do anything she blocked his path and brought the frying pan over the top of his head.

Under the influence of many glasses of liquor, River parked her car and walked up to Dasher's door. First, she knocked softly and then faster and harder until finally, Dasher opened it wide. Wearing only panties and a bra, she was shocked at her body.

"Why you naked?"

"What do you want?" Her eyes were wide, her mannerisms were calm, but River could feel the rage beneath the surface.

River stepped closer. "Aye, um, I—."

"What do you want, River? I'm very busy right now."

"Look, is Mason here?"

"I'm his wife."

She shrugged not knowing what that had to do with anything. "Is he here or not? I'm not playing games!"

"Yes."

She moved to enter. "Good, because I been wanting to talk to him about—."

Dasher blocked her path. "You can't come in my house. I didn't invite you."

River frowned. "If he's in there, why can't I see him? Why can't I come in? I'm not understanding the games."

"You can't come in because I'm protecting him. I'm going to make sure as his wife that nothing happens to him again. And if that means keeping him from you and the Wales' then so be it."

River saw a frying pan on the floor behind her. "What…what happened?"

"Go away, River."

She moved to slam the door, but River stopped her with a flat palm to the surface. "I'm coming back. And if something is wrong with him, if something happened, you'll be dead."

She laughed. "I wonder what Mason would say if he knew you were disrespecting his wife."

"Did you hear me? If you hurting him, you will die. I'll deal with the consequences."

Dasher giggled. "You do what you gotta do. But you ain't getting in my fucking house, dyke!"

SLAM.

Tinsley opened River's bedroom door and watched her sleep from where he stood.

Damn she sexy. He thought as he realized there wasn't much he didn't like about her masculine body.

The tats.

The sports bra.

And even the boxers did something to him that he didn't understand. He was turned on by her swag and he wanted her in his life, even if she wanted no parts of their bond.

As the rain slapped against the windows, he wondered what it would take to convince her to love him. He was prepared to do anything, even if it meant selling his soul.

Because at the end of the day he had to have her.

And he never imagined having feelings for a woman the way he did with her. Sure, he heard of gay men getting women pregnant. It happened a lot. And he reasoned for the act to occur, for them to get hard, they had to see something in the woman that made them reach an orgasm.

With River it was different.

She moved with masculinity.

She wore cologne and she had a personality he found irresistible.

So, the attraction was already there and didn't need to be forced.

Walking over to the bed, he touched her leg lightly. Besides, he knew he could get away with the small act. After all she had been drinking nonstop after being denied access to Mason.

When he touched her leg again and nothing happened, he moved his fingers up to her shin. Next, he touched her thigh and then for some reason he found his fingers peddling the warm space between her legs.

This was the first time he ever touched a woman in that way.

He was never interested.

He wasn't even interested now.

But he wasn't touching some strange woman. He was touching the body of a person he adored. Someone he had grown to love.

When he saw she didn't budge he moved closer, this time inhaling her skin. She smelled of coconut and soap, a surprisingly intoxicating mixture.

The further he went; he was expecting at some point to be disgusted. But that time had yet to arrive.

When he felt the softness between her legs, his stomach buckled. She didn't possess the body he was used to, but she was still his baby. He thought about wanting her and how she took care of him. He thought of her bop and the way she always made him feel safe.

River had been more man to him than his father and it made him want her even more. So, he went further.

Lowering his head between her legs he inhaled.

She smelled clean.

Untouched.

TRUCE 4: THE FINALE 113

And he wanted more. Moving her boxers aside, he lapped between her pussy lips. It was tasteless and a bit moist but different. Suddenly she moved slightly, and he wondered.

Are you really sleep?

And so, he licked again and again until he had done it well over one hundred times. Although her eyes remained closed, he noticed a distinct difference. She was now oily, and he wondered if she enjoyed it.

Yeah, she like this shit. He thought.

Licking a little longer, he flipped his tongue, entered her tunnel, and tickled her clit until he felt her buckle.

She came.

He was sure.

He felt this was the sign that meant things were complete.

Wiping his mouth with the back of his hand, he got up and walked away. Hanging in the doorway he looked down at her and watched her on the bed.

Within seconds she rolled to her side.

He smiled and walked away.

DERRICK

Derrick was lying on the basement floor on top of a mat in the Louisville Estate. Earlier that day Shay placed a weighted blanket on him, and it made his body temperature rise.

The pain he experienced by being struck over the head with a bat was hard to express and he couldn't believe this was his life. Being in agony added to the uneasy emotions he was experiencing by Jersey being missing and his father being shot.

He had no idea what was going on in his world.

He decided to rethink how he dealt with Shay if he was going to get out of the basement. He realized he had to play on her heart.

Because as things stood, his dick itched, he was injured, and Shay was in charge.

CHAPTER NINE

GOD'S EYE

D r. Marjorie Holman decided to have breakfast on her deck. Normally she wasn't the eating outside type of bird, but her companion said the weather was perfect for such an event and he promised to bring over fresh fruit and her favorite champagne to compliment the morning.

He promised to lay the pipe too.

And Old girl was psyched.

Especially since the last thing she heard from him was the laps of her tongue around his dick two days ago under his desk at work. She wanted that man more than a fly wanted shit, so she was hoping for a change of heart.

And so, she wore vibrant loungewear, a hot pink shirt with matching pants. She also ordered fresh buttered croissants and danish as she was far from a cook and knew the treats were his favorite.

Her heartbeat kicked up as the moment neared and a smile stretched across her wrinkled face when she heard her puppy barking inside, indicating that someone was walking alongside the house.

That dog always told tale when a stranger was near that's for sure.

But imagine her surprise when it wasn't her dick delivery that arrived. Instead, she was staring into the shade covered eyes of fine ass Banks Wales. Khaki pants, a white t-shirt and white Gucci's were the outfit of the day.

Oooooh, Dr. Holman was shocked. Afterall, she didn't understand why she was looking at the parent of the child she was overseeing.

And boy did he have an entourage. Six men made the trip, including himself.

And they all held disdain for the woman who wouldn't release the prince.

Calmly Banks walked over a beautiful fruit basket and her favorite champagne before he sat it on the table. "Morning."

She trembled. "Mr. Wales..." she rose, her heart rocking out of her chest. "You shouldn't be at my home. I can schedule an appointment for —."

"Sit."

She remained standing.

"Now."

Slowly she reduced her height into her seat. While his men hung along the sideline like shadows, waiting for his order. To them it was whatever he wanted.

Even death.

"I'm expecting company, Mr. Wales. He'll be here any minute so you can't stay long. You can't hurt me either. People will know. I promise."

"I know you're expecting a guest."

"He won't let you disrespect me and —."

"Who do you think arranged this little meeting?" He took a seat directly in front of her. He smelled good too. Had he not scared her so much, it may have been a nice little brunch with the bachelor.

"So...so he told you to come here?"

Silence.

"He isn't coming?"

"What do you think? But hey, I did bring your champagne."

She finally made the connection and her heart thumped harder with embarrassment. She played the major fool for a man she was clear no longer wanted her. "What do you want?"

"My son. He doesn't belong in that home. We both know it."

"On the contrary. As my colleague explained to you not even three days ago, we believe he does. Do you know I got a report that says he has boys looking away from him as he walks down the hallway? Claiming its disrespectful to look a God in the eyes. That's dangerous rhetoric, Mr. Wales. Which has to be stopped."

"That may be true. But the change he needs won't be done in your facility."

"Mr. Wales, I only have the authority to —."

"Release my boy to me. Don't line up for a war you don't have the armor to endure." He paused. "Stay out of it." He dragged a hand down his face.

"This is not how things are done."

"Then name your price. Because what I know is this, I won't allow him to spend another month in that hole."

"I don't want your money."

"Sure you do. Everybody does."

She shifted in her seat.

"I'll be by on Thursday of next week to get my son. I can make you a millionaire at that time. Or I can make you dead. Your choice."

Slowly he rose leaving her alone. The moment they left she broke into tears. She couldn't believe that Justin set her up in such a way. And she wondered how much money Banks had given him for his betrayal.

Feeling wounded, she dried her eyes with the bottom of her shirt and rose. Popping the champagne, she allowed the coolness to wash down her throat. If nothing else she thought it classy that Banks placed the bottle on chill.

Grabbing the croissants off the table, she walked them inside and came back out to clear the rest of the items.

And then she saw she had new guests.

It was Zantonio, Ziamond, Zuri and Ziggy. The girls were little bruised, but they were more than ready to start another fight. They were also plucking fruit from the platter Banks brought.

Juice from the grapes ran down Zuri's chin and she let it remain like a dog foaming at the mouth.

"I'm Zantonio. And unlike the nigga who just left I'ma make shit real simple. Don't let Ace out of that facility."

"Who are you? You have no right to be in my home!"

"Did you hear me?" Zantonio asked.

"Leave before I —."

Ziamond shot next to the doctor's foot and Marjorie jumped and started crying all over again. She had never experienced so many violent people at once.

Who were these monsters that moved about the world using force and money to get what they wanted?

"Are we clear?" Ziamond said.

"I'll see what I can do."

"Nah, you gonna do it," Zantonio continued. "Or you're dead."

CHAPTER TEN

THE YOUNGEST WALES'

Banks' body melted into the vanilla-colored seats of his Cadillac ESV as he looked down at his padfolio. In less than two weeks he had plans to flee the states and most of his items were checked off.

All except one.

He was trying to keep the show civil, but he had plots to tuck niggas in his favorite spots if they didn't release one of the youngest Wales'.

When the trucked pulled up in front of his house, Banks grabbed his list slipped out and walked toward the mansion. The moment he did River bolted from the bushes while running full speed ahead.

Unfortunately for her she was whacked on the side of the legs by Munro which sent her falling to the ground.

Banks was heated for more than one reason. For starters she should've never made it on the property without one of his men knowing. And secondly, he had zero time for any more of her games.

"Ouch!" She cried rubbing her legs. "Fuck! That shit hurt!"

They removed their weapons and Munro was about to send her to the land of the dead when Banks raised his hand. "Don't."

They froze.

Weapons tucked back against their bodies.

Lowering his height, he knelt as River moaned in pain. "Does it hurt?"

"Fuck you think?" She yelled rubbing her throbbing legs. "Shit, you didn't have to do that!"

He chuckled once and grew serious. "It could've been worse." He lifted his shades. "Never run up on me again. Ever." He rose and looked at Munro. "Pick her up and carry her in the house."

Munro scooped her and flung her over his shoulder like a backpack. When it came to strength the man appeared to have superhero abilities.

Once inside, River sat on the sofa icing her legs while Banks sat in his recliner across the way, eyeing her closely. "You're loyal," he said. "I can see that."

She looked at the bruise and put the ice back in place. "It ain't like that."

"What is it like then?"

She sighed and breathed deeply. "I don't like to see people I love hurt. I'm sure you would do the same thing if it were somebody you cared about."

"Somebody hurt?"

"Yes."

"What the fuck are you talking about?"

"Banks, I been calling you nonstop."

He shrugged. "And?"

"You didn't return any of my calls."

"We not friends. And even if we were, if you don't tell me what you want directly, you'll never get a call back. Now what are you talking about?"

"I think...I mean, I don't have any facts, but I think Mason may be hurt."

Banks sat his glass down and shifted.

"And I need your help. I know you don't like me. Probably don't trust me either but I ain't got no place else to go."

"He was shot. Of course, he's hurt."

"I mean he's not in the hospital no more. And I haven't been able to contact nobody to see if he's cool."

"What exactly do you think I can do?"

"This is going to sound crazy and I'm sorry. But I'm pretty sure Dasher is doing something weird to him."

Banks frowned. "Weird like what?"

"Earlier I went past the house and asked to see him. She said he was home, but she wouldn't let him see me. And...I mean...I saw a frying pan on the floor. The shit

was mad out of place. Now I know she's his wife but—
."

"Wife?" He glared.

"Yeah. They got married on some shotgun shit right before he was shot. He didn't tell you?"

Silence.

"Anyway, I was there when they got married and I could've sworn he didn't wanna do it. It's like he did it just to have somebody in his life you know? And now he's shot and she's responsible for everything regarding his health. But—."

"Let me stop you. I don't care about none of the shit you spitting. The only thing on my mind is getting my son."

"Banks, please."

"If he married her that means he trusts her with his life. And I suggest you do yourself a favor and stay out of their business. Whatever you do, leave me the fuck out of it."

A baby cried incessantly to the left in the waiting room.

Minnesota and Spacey sat nervously at the OBGYN's office to speak about the discomfort she was experiencing while trying to carry full term. Although her mind was on her unborn child and Zercy, his thoughts were with Lila who was blowing his ear up on the other end of the phone.

Ever since they separated, and he kept Riot for most of the time she grew evil. Looking for any possible way to rattle him and get Riot back.

So far nothing worked.

"He is my son," she said anxiously into the cell. "I gave birth to him, not you. And I'm tired of this game."

"And I told you I know you're his mother." He grabbed a magazine and flipped and flipped through pages with his free hand. Just to have something to do. "You don't have to keep telling me."

"So why do you barely let me see him? And when I do, lately he's been surrounded by security. What's going on?"

Spacey sat back and sighed.

Banks increased security around all of them lately, even though they thought they were inconspicuous. "That's my father's doing."

"Don't play with me, Spacey. I know you have something to do with it too. Riot is a boy. He needs to be around his mother. I would never hurt him."

"Is everything okay?" Minnesota whispered nudging Spacey softly on the arm.

He smiled and nodded yes.

It wasn't.

"Look, I'm busy right now, Lila. I said what I said, and we'll have to leave it at that for now." He sighed. "I'll call you later when—."

"Was that Minnesota's voice I just heard?" She said with disdain. "Your sister slash girlfriend?"

He sat up. "Be careful."

"Spacey, I know you don't have respect for me. And I also know your family is powerful. But there is no way in the world that I will allow you to keep him. He's mine. He's all I got. Without him I can't breathe."

"Well, I guess you gonna suffocate then, bitch." He hung up.

Two hours later, after seeing the doctor, they were back at Minnesota's house. Both were eating fruit at the table in the kitchen because lately she could only keep down the freshest of meals.

While they ate, she looked up at him and grinned.

"Why you looking at me like that?" He laughed.

"I wanna ask you something but I don't want you to get mad."

He chuckled. "Okay…shoot."

"Did it hurt?"

"What you talking about?"

"When Howard raped you?"

Fruit, a grape, toppled on the floor. "What did you, what did you just say? Huh? We were having a good conversation and you —."

"I know, Spacey. No need to lie to me. Besides, you and I have shared more things together than any siblings ever could or should. I'm really asking because I want to know. Not because I want to hurt you."

Spacey felt queasy.

It was the type of sensation that made him want to get violent. It matched the energy of embarrassment running through his soul.

"How did you...how...did you know?"

"I heard Pops asking you if it were true. When we were at the house last week. I was in the bathroom down in the basement and both of you were talking about the situation. He told you that Mason brought it up and he was sorry you had to go through that. I really wasn't being nosey, but I felt it would be bad taste to come out at that time."

"Well, if you heard us talking then you also heard me tell him no."

"You did. But I know you."

He flopped back. "I wish you never said you were there." Spacey grabbed a grape and pressed it with two fingers until its juice squirted on the table.

"What he did...what I allowed him to do was at a time I barely recognize anymore," Spacey continued. "It was when I was a different man. I changed. And nobody or nothing will ever violate me in that way again. And that's all you need to know."

She smiled. "Okay."

He inhaled and exhaled. "Anyway, are you ready to leave all this shit behind and go to our island?"

Silence.

"Minnie..."

"What?"

"Are you ready or not?"

"I'm not going." She exhaled.

First, she hit him with a right with the rape question and then she followed up with a left with the news of her not going to the island. Something they talked about repeatedly. Especially after Banks let them see the beautiful land.

Who wouldn't want to go and escape America?

Between the two blows he wasn't sure if he would be able to handle his rage.

"Why would you stay here?" He tossed his hands up. "Ain't shit about this country good, Minnie. The plan was to always bounce you know that."

"I know but—."

"But what?"

"My child's father is here, Spacey."

He really felt like swinging now. "So, the fuck what? You said he lied to you."

"He didn't lie. He held things back."

"Same thing!"

"Spacey, I can't have my baby growing up without a father. Life is different without two parents. You know that! I want my baby to have a chance at a normal life. Something we never had."

His eyes lowered. "I can't let you stay here. You understand that right?"

"Let me?"

Silence.

"Spacey, you don't have a choice. My decision is already made. And if you love me like you claim you do, then you'll stay out of it. Okay?"

He sat back in the chair, grabbed a handful of grapes and squished them until he made wine.

Mason sat in his wheelchair in the center of Dasher's bedroom. In an effort to spice up the relationship, she lowered the lights and put on some old school music. Jodeci led the way.

But what she wanted the moment to give was coming up short. Because she could've been a roach on the wall and Mason would have the same response.

Utter disgust.

Dancing up to him slowly she smiled as she gyrated her hips in a winding fashion. In the first place she couldn't dance and in the second place he wanted to throw up in his mouth as he watched her attempts to be sexy.

At one point he did lust after her, but now, well, he hated her guts.

Stooping down, she got on her knees and stroked his penis to a thickness. As hard as she worked, and she did work hard, it remained as limp as a gummy worm.

She grew heated.

"What's wrong with it?" She looked down at it as if it were a dead animal.

He shrugged. "I don't feel like it."

She glared. "You don't feel like it? What the fuck is that supposed to mean?"

"I don't want to have sex with you, Dasher."

She looked at him and laughed. "Mason, you always wanna fuck. And the doctor said your situation doesn't mean you aren't able to have sex. So, stop playing and get in the mood for—."

"I don't wanna fuck you!" He yelled. "Period!"

"Yeah okay. We'll see about that."

Thinking it was a game, she crawled on top of him and moved her crusty panties to the side. Grabbing his limp dick, she sat on top of it and hit the surfboards. After gyrating, spinning and turning that box, his dick got tinier.

Angry, she sat on top of him in the wheelchair and glared. "I hate you. Do you know that? I fucking hate you."

"Listen, I'm not in the mood to—."

SMACK!

Mason wanted to choke her out.

"You think you gonna stay in my house, have the ability to fuck me and don't take the pussy? What's the use of having you around if you don't satisfy me? You should be giving up the dick and eating the pussy too."

I wish I would. He thought.

"You don't want to be married to me, Dasher. You hate me. You've made that clear several times. Open the door and let me go."

Silence.

"Let me go, Dasher. Give me my son and —."

Now she heard him.

"Even if I pushed you out of this house, I would never let you take Bolt with you. Ever! Do you understand? I'll kill you first!"

Suddenly Mason felt warm liquid on his waist. When he looked down, he saw she pissed on him.

"I guess I was able to release after all."

He glared. "You gonna wish you never did that shit to me."

"Stay in the chair for the rest of the night. Maybe you'll get some sense about yourself and learn to respect me."

Mason wasn't a praying man. But in that moment, he wished for her death.

And he wanted it as painful as possible too.

CHAPTER ELEVEN

THE FOULEST SHIT

Banks was driving down the street when he saw a familiar face parked next to his car at the light. She was driving a red Benz and her vanilla-colored skin was painted lightly as her blonde hair flirted with the wind.

"Joanne," he said rolling down the window.

Wondering where the voice came from, she looked over at him, her eyes widened, and then her mouth dropped in disbelief. "Blaire? Is that you?"

He smiled and shook his head. "Nah, shawty. I'm a long ways away from Blaire. But pull into that parking lot up there though."

She quickly did as instructed and within a minute they were standing face to face. Joanne was in fucking disbelief and awe. The last time Banks saw Joanne she was Blaire, and Joanne was her best good girlfriend.

Since then, the hormone therapy had caught up and now Banks had returned to his former glory. For a second, he thought about the past. Banks remembered her trying hard back in the day to convince him that Mason shouldn't be trusted. And now Banks was realizing that she was right all along.

Joanne stepped closer. "Blaire, you look—."

"Banks." He corrected her leaning against his car. "My name is Banks."

"Oh, I'm sorry, I...I didn't mean to disrespect I just—."

"No disrespect taken. Just letting you know."

"I can't...wow...you look different."

"It's who I always was. I was lied to by Mason and those around me and now I'm putting back the pieces of my life."

She nodded. "Well...you look...very good. I can hardly even see Blaire anymore." Her eyes roamed over his body. "Your hair, the five o'clock shadow...the way you move...all...different."

Banks caught the meaning behind her words. At the end of the day the woman that was once his best friend wanted to fuck him straight up.

"Listen, I asked you to pull over because, well, I wanted to say that you were right."

"About what?" She moved closer.

"Mason. I had no business being around him and...let's just say I lost a lot of time dealing with him. Time I can never get back."

"I'm so sorry."

"Why?"

"Because I saw how much you cared about him. And—."

"It wasn't like that."

"I don't understand."

"I didn't care about him in a romantic way. He was a friend of mine who took advantage of my memory loss and told me I was his wife."

She covered her mouth with her fingertips. "His wife! What? Are you serious?"

"Yeah. He did the foulest shit ever imagined and now it's about me putting things back in order."

"I'm torn."

"Why you say that?"

"Because had he not come back for you, even with lying, you wouldn't have found out who you are. I mean I love your grandmother; you know we were close before she passed but she never would have told you about your history."

"He still went about it the wrong way. He's—."

"I know he was wrong. I do. But I saw him a few times at Strong Curls, Banks. He cares about you. And even though I'm your friend—."

"At one point you wanted me sexually. So how do I know I can trust you?"

"I still want you now. That's probably what I sensed when I was around you."

"Wow. I see you taking charge of what you're feeling these days."

"I'm done denying the truth." She paused. "I have and will always be attracted to you. But you don't want me and that's something I have to deal with." She sighed. "Still that man cared. Intentions be damned, and I felt I needed to say that."

"Well, I don't want anybody around me who..." Suddenly a pressure ripped through Banks' head. It was so heavy that it rocked him to the ground.

"Banks, are you okay?" She asked looking down at him.

He wasn't.

In fact, the pain was so wicked it was blinding, and he had to lower his head to stop some of the thump.

"I need you to do me a favor," he said gripping the sides of his face.

"Sure, anything."

"Get me to the hospital. Something is wrong."

As Banks sat on the hospital bed in the emergency room, Joanne continued to take looks at him on a sly. She didn't mean to be so creepy, but she couldn't get over how handsome he was.

"Stop staring, Joanne," he said holding the sides of his head.

"I'm...I'm sorry. Can I get you anything?"

"Nah...just want some answers." He paused. "If something happens though, tell my family the plan remains intact. And that they should go along with everything outlined in our meetings. They will know what I mean."

"Sure. Anything."

Two hours later a doctor entered the room, with a serious expression on his face. "We have some answers, Mr. Wales."

Banks nodded.

"It appears you may be having some issues with the brain surgery you underwent awhile back. And the complications are as a direct result of the hormone therapy."

"Wait, so you're saying the therapy is bad?"

"I'm not saying the therapy is bad. I'm saying that its wrong for you."

"Can you be clearer?" Joanne asked when she noticed he was at a loss for words. "Because this is all so sudden."

"He's going to have to stop using the medication. Immediately."

Banks fell backwards into the bed. There was no way in the world he could see not being his true self.

The therapy contributed directly to his reconnecting with the past. And to hear he was going to have to give that up was unacceptable.

For some reason he thought about the pastor's words too.

Was this his karma?

"Stop using the...what will happen to me? I'm...I'm..." he was having difficulty saying trans since the mentioning of the word was still far off from who he felt like inside. "I need this therapy to be who I am."

"I understand, but if you continue things will get worse, Mr. Wales."

"What does that mean exactly?" Joanne asked.

The doctor took a deep breath, clearly trying to avoid the truth. "Mr. Wales, based on your brain scans, you either stop the therapy or you will be dead outside of a month."

RIVER

River drove down the street in silence despite Tinsley being in the car, wanting more than anything to talk to her. To connect with her. To have a talk about the emotions he was willing to accept. But she wasn't interested in *the* conversation.

Her mind and heart were elsewhere.

His mind was on the sexual experience they shared the other night.

"Are you going to let me in, River?"

She stopped at the light and then sighed. She forgot another human was in the car. "What you just say?"

"River, what's going on?"

"Nothing." She frowned while also shaking her head from left to right. "Why you keep asking me that?" She leaned back in the seat.

He sighed. "You mean besides the fact that you've said less than two words to me since we reconnected?"

"I told you I had shit going on. You thought it was a game."

"You know what, it's whatever at this point. Basically, I just want you to know that I'm leaving soon."

Silence.

"River, did you hear me?"

"Uh…nah."

"I said I'm leaving soon."

She sighed. "You told me that already. And when you did, I told you that if you aren't willing to give me details, I really don't care."

"Wow."

"Listen, I hate to be so cold but—."

"What do you need, River?"

"Stop with all the mind games."

"It's not a mind game. Ever since you haven't spoken to Mason you been cold. And you wasn't that talkative to begin with, so things are really bad now. So, I'm asking you what do you need from me? So that I can get my friend back."

She looked at him before putting eyes back on the road. "You won't be able to do nothing."

"Try me."

She sighed.

In the back of her mind, she was sure her situation was out of the realm of help. But what did she have to lose? Banks had made a decision that the only thing he was interested in was bringing Ace home. And his men, who Mason hired, were also not interested.

"I want to find out something on Dasher. I got a feeling that something is off, but I don't know what."

"Okay, give me more."

"Like, I mean, I need to get her background. I don't know nothing about her and to be honest, I'm not sure Mason really knows her either. He was so desperate to make her his wife. Like he was trying to force a family and shit."

"You really do care about him don't you?"

She looked over at him. "You gonna help me or not?"

"I got a friend who can get you any information you need on anybody. His name is Emo. Maybe we should head over his house."

Shay stood over Derrick with her arms folded tightly against her body. He claimed he was still in pain, but she didn't believe him.

He was a liar.

And she knew this because since she struck him, she had been through every aspect of his phone. And boy did she find a lot about him. Including details of his relationship with Natty, which she always suspected.

The hate she had for him was sincere.

And growing by the second text message read.

"Baby, what are you going to do?" He moaned as his body lay on top of the floor pallet, she made for him days ago. "I mean, have you thought this through? You can't hit a person over the head and possibly give them HIV and that be that. I feel like something else might be wrong, Shay. I mean do you love me or not?"

"Did you think things through before you fucked that bitch Flower?" She yelled. "Or Natty?"

He blinked many times.

"Oh yeah, I went through your phone, nigga. I know all about it."

"Shay, I know I was wrong. I swear I do. But I was stupid. I didn't realize how much you meant to me. Plus, we were having problems and — ."

"You a dirty dick ass nigga. Just like your father."

He sighed. "Shay, my head doesn't feel right. I'm not sure if I'm even going to make it. Do you really wanna be responsible for killing me?"

"What was it about her? What was it about them? Huh? That you would do this to me. Help me understand because I'm confused." Huge tear droplets fell from her eyes and dampened her shirt.

"They didn't mean anything."

"That's worse. Because at least if they meant something to you, I would understand why you jeopardized our marriage."

Suddenly he tried to get comfortable on the floor, but it wouldn't work. A mixture of guilt and pain terrorized him.

"I get Natty, but why Flower?"

"Don't do this, Shay."

"WHY DID YOU FUCK FLOWER?!"

He swallowed the lump in his throat. "Okay, at Christmas, the next day after the party, when she came over with River, she was really nice."

"You mean the first time we all met her?" She glared.

"Yes. She kept talking about how scared she was to meet everybody. And how she wanted a friend. None of ya'll would talk to her so I...I—."

"Gave her some dick?"

"Nah, we just grew close. Before I knew it, we exchanged numbers and—."

"ARRRRRRHHHHHHHHHHGGHHHHHHHH!" Shay screamed holding her head. "JUST SHUT UP! JUST SHUT UP! JUST SHUT THE FUCK UP, NIGGA!"

He knew in that moment that he said too much. All of it was a trap and he figured it was just a matter of time before she killed him. "Shay...please don't do anything stupid."

"You were all I had and you...you didn't care. You never cared about me, did you?" She stepped closer and it was at that time that he saw she was carrying the bat once again.

How did he miss it?

"Of course, I cared about you. I married you!"

"Then why would you go outside of our marriage for strangers? I'm not understanding! You destroyed everything we had together. Everything!"

He saw she was growing more enraged, and he realized she didn't want answers to prevent killing him. She wanted to be mad enough to commit murder.

There was a major difference.

"You want me to sit down here and act like you didn't have everything to do with why I fucked both of them bitches?"

"What you just say?"

"You heard me! You want to pretend like I didn't beg you to focus on our marriage and our son all those days you concerned yourself with what Banks was doing? You want to pretend like I didn't beg you to focus just a little time on our marriage? Well, I'm not about to do it. Yeah, I smashed them hoes! Bof' of 'em. But you were just as much to blame as me. And if you don't see that, I don't give a fuck no more."

In that instance he gave her everything she needed.

And so, she brought the bat down over his head once more.

Mason could hear her breathing as he lie in bed as stiff as a Barbie.

Lately every time he woke up, she was in the kitchen cooking some exotic meal in an effort to woo him over with food. And when he didn't tell her how amazing she was she grew angry and would throw something at him. Unlike the frying pan that she brought directly over his head on day one, usually she would miss during these bouts.

But she was growing more volatile.

Still, this was the first time he was up before her and as a result, he would have access to the house. This wasn't by chance. Instead of drinking the tea she gave him at the end of each day, claiming it would make him relax, last night he refused. He suspected she was drugging him.

He was right.

And so, as he heard her snores, he quietly pushed himself out of his bed and toward the right where his chair was normally parked. But he made a great mistake. He didn't look, and as a result he hit the floor.

THUMP.

She moved my chair. He thought as he lie face down on the floor. *Stupid bitch!*

Suddenly the bed shook.

She turned over.

He had to remain still. Unfortunately, his breathing was so heavy he placed his hands over his mouth to stop his own breath. The fact that he was scared of his own wife worried him in ways he'd never worried before.

It seemed like forever but finally he heard her snoring and so he slowly and carefully released the hold he had on his mouth.

When he raised his head, and looked straight ahead, he could see the chair in the hallway. Using his upper body strength, which was limited due to being shot along with stress, he dragged himself toward his chair.

One arm down.

Pull.

Second arm down.

Pull.

He repeated the process until his body was halfway in the hallway and the other half was in the bedroom.

And then he saw it.

The item he really wanted.

His phone was sitting on the floor while being charged in the wall. He had to get it to call for help. He contemplated leaving his wheelchair and using the strength he had left to get his phone instead, but would he make it?

And so, he remained still.

While actively listening, to be certain she was asleep. Because if he were going to take the effort, he had to be sure.

The silence was killing him and then he heard her soft snore.

She was asleep.

He still had time!

He decided to ditch the chair and crawl a little more. It was hell, but five minutes later he managed to pull himself all the way to his phone. His heart thumbed from exhaustion and fear as he grabbed his cell.

Sweating and leaning against the wall, he called Derrick's number first.

No answer.

Fuck! He thought.

Sure, he could've called the authorities. But he knew he had at least a key in the basement of Dasher's house. Something he planned to get rid of after making her his wife. The last thing he needed was some cop snooping around even though it would be fruit of the poisonous tree if they found the cocaine.

Nah, the police were out.

He even thought about trying Banks, but he didn't want him focusing on his situation when he knew he was trying to get Ace out of the facility.

And so, he called the one woman who put him in the position in the first and second place.

Jersey.

She didn't answer.

The man was at his phone and *still* couldn't get help!

Feeling like he would miss his moment and get caught, he remembered the nurse at the hospital programmed her number before he left.

At the time he thought it was innocent but with hindsight and retrospect he realized that maybe, just maybe, there was a method to her madness. It was a great possibility that she was interested in him.

Could she help?

Scanning through the phone, he located her number. He was just about to hit send when he heard Bolt crying.

Fuck. He thought to himself.

Suddenly, Dasher, half sleep, ran out of the room barefoot toward Bolt's room. She didn't turn her head to the right and so she didn't see him sitting on the floor against the wall.

Quickly he pressed send and when the nurse answered he said, "Adrenna, it's me. Listen...I need —."

"Who's me?"

"Mason Louisville." He whispered. "You put your number in the phone when…"

It was too late.

Dasher walked toward him with Bolt in her arms. The baby's feet were dangling as they both stared at him below. And Mason, a grown man, had never been more terrified in all his life.

Removing the phone from his hand she placed it against her ear. "Who is this?" She asked while holding the baby who was smiling down at Mason.

He wiped sweat from his brow.

"Can you put Mason back on the phone?" Adrenna asked.

"No, I can't. This is his wife. Now who is this?"

"Oh, I'm sorry. I remember you. I didn't mean any disrespect."

"Are you sure about that? Because anybody who doesn't mean disrespect would not have my man's number."

"Ma'am, I'm the nurse. He sounded upset and I want to make sure he's okay. Nothing more or less."

"He's fine. And even if he wasn't he don't need you."

Mason, deciding to speak up yelled, "No, I'm not okay. This bitch is — ."

What Dasher did next made him realize he had no business marrying her at all. Suddenly the things she did in the past that he thought was cute added to the narrative that she was crazier than he was prepared to understand.

From pissing on him in the wheelchair, the blowjobs while he was shitting on the toilet, to stealing his sperm and shooting it in herself using a turkey baster. Everything led to the moment in which she pressed the face of the baby into her breasts, in an attempt to suffocate him.

"Like I said, he's fine right, Mason?" Dasher said fully prepared to kill her own child.

Silence.

"Mason, aren't you fine?"

Seeing his baby boy dying before his eyes changed everything. "I'M FINE!" He yelled. "I'M...I'M FINE."

"You heard him? We're fine."

Dasher smiled, hung up and released the child who took a deep breath.

"Don't fuck with me, Mason. I'm not one of them stupid ass whores you got with in the past. I will kill everybody up in this bitch. Including this damn baby."

She walked away as the child cried in her arms.

The preacher was right.

Mason Louisville had entered hell.

CHAPTER TWELVE

FRUIT

A ce sat in the lunchroom quietly.

His head rotated slowly from left to right and if you asked the child directly, he could accurately tell you where every adult was posted up in the room. Although they were hired to look after troubled children in the boy's home, most of the employees were too young to be of any real service. Reliable staff may have prevented many issues, but hindsight was always twenty-twenty, and nobody gave a fuck bout' 'dem kids.

What a shame.

Because across the room Ace spotted Mathew Miller.

His next victim.

Matthew was a young child who just arrived and for some reason was still in possession of his necklace. This perplexed the Wales spawn because he was immediately relieved of all his dressings the moment he stepped through the doors.

So why he get to keep his stuff? Ace pondered, as he looked upon the cheap piece with malice in his heart.

Sure, the chain wasn't anything like the diamond studded jewels that rested around his neck prior to entering the home. All the Wales twins' jewelry was custom-made and cost over one hundred grand per flex.

But still, the way the light hit the gold chain Matthew wore made Ace want it for himself.

Besides, wasn't it better to have some jewelry than none at all?

Slowly Ace eased out of his seat and walked toward him. When he made it to the table, he pulled out the chair, hopped in and sat directly across from him.

"You new?" Ace smiled.

Matthew looked at him and then looked away. He heard of the things Ace would do if stared at too long.

"Yeah," he focused on his cereal.

"You like it here?"

"No."

Ace nodded. "How come you get to keep that?" He pointed at the necklace.

"Keep what?" He asked, eyes still low.

"Your chain."

He shrugged. "I don't know."

"My chain better than yours."

"So, where is it?"

"They took it. And now I don't have one." He looked at the chain a bit harder.

"So." He shrugged again. He attempted to focus on his meal, but his stomach did somersaults as he tried to be a "big boy" like his social worker suggested.

"So, give it to me." Ace placed his hands together on top of the table. "I want it."

Now he looked upon Ace directly. "No."

As Ace glared, two boys had placed their pieces of fruit in front of him on the table, a demand given to them after Ace set a few bullies straight early on. But he wasn't interested in their gifts in the moment.

He wanted the chain.

"Give it here." He demanded again. It was more like a warning than a request.

"I said no."

"Okay."

Ace smiled, got up and walked away.

Matthew looked at him the entire time wondering what he would do next. When he saw Ace whisper in a bigger kid's ear, only for that same kid to approach him seconds later, immediately he grew frightened.

Standing next to him, the boy's meaty hand opened, and he glared. "Give it to me."

From across the room Ace smiled.

Matthew may have felt like he could take on Ace, but this kid was taller, wider and could easily pass for a middle schooler. And so, he unlatched the necklace, dropped it in his palm and cried.

Ace smiled as he waited across the cafeteria for his delivery.

Banks' headache was unrelenting.

And he was certain, that if it didn't stop that he would be forced to go to the emergency room again. Some place he wasn't interested in returning. At the same time not using his hormone therapy was out of the question.

In his mind he already wasted time with Mason believing he was a woman and so he was willing to die to live as he desired.

Even if it meant he only had months.

As he bypassed his own security to pull up in front of Morgan's house, who was one of his nanny's, he parked.

Ever since Ace had been approached by his aunt before the butler killed her, he didn't feel comfortable with leaving them unsecured. So, wherever his kids were, armed men were too.

After all, that one incident resulted in Ace being taken from the family.

Banks even had security at the troubled boys home as well as staff members who were on payroll. They never made themselves known, instead they hung in the corners ready to do Banks' bidding.

"Come in, Banks," Morgan smiled when she opened the door. "Walid just finished breakfast."

Banks stepped inside and sat on the sofa. "Uh, thank you. Do you have everything you need?"

"Of course," she smiled.

He nodded.

"Banks, sir, I...can I call you Banks?"

"Banks is fine."

She smiled. "I wanted to tell you that I haven't, well, I haven't heard from Mason." She paused. "And I'm worried. When I lived with him, he was always in the children's lives. He even called a few times a day when the twins lived with him and I stayed at the house. I think something maybe wrong. We should — ."

"Morgan, I'm not trying to hear about no Mason right now." He waved the air across her face.

"I understand, I really do." She stepped closer. "It's just that, well, I remember."

"I remember now too." He glared. "A lot." He sat back. "And the more my memory returns, the angrier I get for him trying to pass our relationship off as anything other than friendship."

"He was definitely wrong to do that to you."

"Wrong is an understatement."

"You're correct." She paused. "We all played a part in the deceit. I should've said something too, but I didn't know how."

"Morgan, what do you want?"

"It's just that, not hearing from him is so out of character. Mr. Louisville may have made some sly moves but one thing he always did was check on his sons. Especially the younger ones. As a matter of fact, since he quit drinking, he made even more effort to be in their lives."

Banks was irritated. "They aren't his sons."

"I didn't mean it that way."

"Morgan, Mason is married."

Her eyes widened. "Married?"

He nodded his head. "So, he didn't bother telling you that part?"

"No...um...he didn't."

"Well, he married Dasher. And maybe she doesn't want him around everyone. It's her right. It ain't like

Jersey didn't shoot him. Dasher could be in protective mode."

She looked down. "Banks, I wish — ."

"Morgan, I let you watch Walid because I trust you around him. You should consider that an honor because there are very few people in my life right now, I can say that about." He rose. "But when it comes to Mason and me, do yourself a favor and stay out of it. Now bring me Walid."

As she went to scoop his son, Banks received a call from his head of security. "Sir, you were right, there were many threats made on your family. It's all been isolated at this point."

"Any ideas on who it may have been?"

"We are making some inquiries now. I'll have an answer for you in a few days."

"Make it one."

CHAPTER THIRTEEN

THE RAPE

Minnie sat on the toilet and slapped at the tissue roll. When she wiped herself, she saw blood. Her eyes widened as a sinking feeling took over her soul. Was she about to lose her baby? After all she was in her first trimester and never wanted anything as much as she did her unborn child. And yet a part of her soul felt like she wasn't worthy of bringing a life into this world.

Later that day, she visited the doctor and was given the run down.

"The baby is fine, Minnesota. But you must go on bedrest. This is so important that it can't be understated."

Minnesota's eyes widened. "So am I...will I..."

"You can have a healthy labor but like I said you'll need help. Can you call anyone to wait on you hand and foot?"

She thought about telling Banks. But if she did, she was certain he would have all kinds of people crawling around. She would never have any free time.

And if she tapped her own banking account, that he replenished, to hire a nurse, he would still detect a problem.

She needed help but she had to go another route.

So, after returning home she made a call.

Help came right away.

Zercy was in the kitchen preparing toast buttered on one side with a hint of garlic for taste. It was one of Minnie's favorite snacks and he needed her to have every desire. Bringing the meal to her with a side of orange juice, he sat on the edge of the bed as she ate.

"Thank you," she said as he placed the breakfast tray over her legs. "I'm starving." She smiled.

"That's a good sign."

"I hope so." She took a tiny bite and sat it down. "Zercy, do you think I mean, are you sure I will be —."

"Don't say it."

She frowned. "How do you know what I'm about to say?"

"You were going to ask if I think our baby will be okay."

She looked down.

He sat closer while being careful to give her space. "Minnesota Wales, you not only will bring this baby to full term, but when the baby arrives you will be the best mother ever."

She shook her head. "You can't say that."

"I'm serious. You will love this baby and you will be a wonderful mother. You have to believe it because it's true."

"I hope so."

He winked and rubbed her knee.

"You know you can't stay right?"

He removed his hand. "I know."

"I need more time."

"Minnie…"

"Don't, Zercy."

"Let me finish. I know so much has happened between us. And I know trust is a thing of the past. But I need you to realize that there is nothing I won't do to repair our relationship. It's not a mistake that I've come into your life—."

"Please stop."

"Why?"

"Because I'm tired of the words. I'm tired of you telling me the things I want to hear. Until I feel one hundred percent comfortable that your family won't interfere in our lives, I want nothing to do with you."

"Nothing?"

"You heard me."

"So, what am I doing here then, Minnie? Huh? Why invite me here if you don't want me around."

She glared. "Zercy, I need a nurse. I have the money, but I don't want to use my card because I don't want my father finding out and worrying even more."

"I can do that for you. No problem. I can pay for it too. So don't —."

"Like I said, I have the money. I just —."

"Minnie, it's my baby too. If you need help let me help. Okay?"

"You don't care that in the beginning you won't be around?"

"I should be grateful you even let me be here tonight. It's hard to be around you and not touch you. Not support you when…"

HIS PHONE RANG.

He removed it from his pocket and from Minnie's view, she could see it was Ziamond, his sister.

She looked away.

After all, she'd seen enough.

They were annoying as fuck.

His finger hovered over the answer button, preparing to take the call but he stopped. Suddenly his heart was filled with rage, something he hadn't allowed himself to feel in years. And so, he ignored the call, stuffed it into his pocket and focused back on her.

"Just so you know, nothing else matters but you. And over the next few months, you will see. I — ."

A TEXT MESSAGE.

He dug in his pocket to retrieve the cell again and read it.

Ziamond: PLEASE HIT ME BACK. I WAS

RAPED.

His heart jumped.

Fear rang across his expression.

Worried, Minnesota sat up and touched his hand. "Zercy, are you okay?"

Silence.

"Zercy, what's wrong? You're scaring me."

He was preparing to get up, rush out of the house and run to his family's aid. Something he had done ever since his parents died. Whenever the triplets needed him, since Zantonio was for the streets, he was always there.

And because of it, he lost Minnesota.

He stood up, placed the phone on the dresser and walked over to the bed. Sitting back down he said, "Everything is fine. You need anything else?"

She smiled, grabbed her toast and took a larger bite. "Nah, I'm good."

THE TRIPLETS

The triplets stood in Ziamond's apartment and looked at one another. Tossing the phone down,

Ziamond walked away from her sisters and leaned against the wall in her living room. "He didn't answer his phone." Her gaze was fixed as tears rolled down her cheek. "He didn't answer his fucking phone!"

"I thought you said after he popped up over here, that we should just give him his space for a couple of days." Zuri said. "And that he would get over it."

"Why is he ignoring us?" Ziggy added. "What did we do to him to be treated like this?"

"I told ya'll not to push him!" Zuri yelled, walking over to the bar to pour herself a large glass of wine. "Didn't I?"

"Oh, so it's our fault now?" Ziamond said. "Because if I can remember you didn't want him around that red bitch either."

"We have always been there for him! When his first girlfriend died, who picked up behind him?" Ziggy asked. "Who cooked all his meals? We did."

"It doesn't matter!" Zuri continued. "Had we not killed her, maybe we would still have him in our lives and —."

"I think you are very absent minded," Ziamond said pointing her way. "It was your idea to take her out on that boat and drown her. Not ours!"

Upon hearing the truth Zuri flopped on the sofa an dragged a hand down her face. "If I lose my brother I—."

"We won't lose him." Ziamond said.

"But how can you be sure?"

"Because just like we took out his last girlfriend and he came back to us, we can take out this bitch too." Ziamond continued. "Whoever Zantonio got working for him not moving fast enough. We have to focus on just the girl."

"I can't go through that again," Zuri said.

"Me either." Ziggy responded. "And I thought you said we would leave her alone until the baby was born."

"I did."

"So, what changed?" Zuri asked.

"Are you that stupid?"

She glared.

"This bitch is trying to ruin our lives. This bitch is trying to destroy our world and I won't let the fact that our brother nutted up in her demolish shit. It may bring up too many things we need to stay quiet."

"So, what now?" Ziggy asked.

"We make the call again."

"To Zantonio?"

"Who else?"

CHAPTER FOURTEEN

LIKE A KINGPIN

B anks, Spacey and Joey sat on the deck of Banks' home drinking whiskey, smoking cigars and talking all things paradise island. Soft rap played in the background even though not one of them were listening.

"...so, if we stick to the plan things should go smoothly," Banks said flicking ash off his tip.

Spacey sighed. "Do you have any reason to think things won't go as planned?" He pulled and released smoke into the air.

Banks sighed. "I don't think so. At the same time there are so many different pieces that we must consider. What I want you to do is remember the plan." He pointed at each of them with the tip. "I've gone over every detail with you both. We can't have any mistakes.

And if something happens to me, I need everybody on that jet. So don't—"

"Are you okay?" Joey asked out of concern.

"Yes, son. I'm fine."

Joey nodded and sat back. "Can I...I mean...can I ask you what's with so much security?"

"What do you mean?"

"Me and my wife have spotted strange people following us and hanging around the house lately. At first it was a car or two but now it's out of control."

"And?"

"Pops, I don't want to scare my wife off. She barely knows about me and my past. The security is given drug dealer vibes and—."

"I don't deal in that lifestyle anymore."

"I know, Pops. But you move like a kingpin."

Banks sat the cigar in the tray and leaned closer. He knew firsthand that attempts had been made on all their lives, but he didn't want to strike more fear in their hearts.

"Listen, I need you all safe. And I'll do what I must to see that this happens. Because for some reason, I feel a dark energy around us."

"We are safe. Since we don't deal anymore, nobody is looking for us."

"That may be true, but I'm not taking any chances." The new butler stepped up to them and refreshed their whiskey glasses. "And I'm sorry if that's hard to understand but nothing will stop me from reaching my goal."

Joey may have been a little put off by security but Spacey was grinning. The way Banks handled business let him know that he was even closer to being the man he remembered.

Which lately was all he wanted.

"Okay, Pops," Joey sighed. "Whatever you say. Can you have them be a little more inconspicuous maybe?"

Banks thought for a moment. "I'll talk to them."

Joey nodded. "Thanks, Pops."

"There are a few other things I want to discuss." Spacey said. "What do we do if one of us decides we aren't going?"

Joey glared. "Fuck is you saying? We making all these moves and you don't want to go?"

"I never said it was me."

"Then who are you referring to?" Joey pressed.

Spacey wanted to tell them that he was speaking of Minnesota but the last thing he wanted was to make her hate him even more.

"Uh, Shay."

"Shay is thinking about staying?" Joey frowned. "For what?"

"I don't know." He shrugged. "I stopped by to see her the other day and she barely wanted to let me in the house."

Joey nodded. "I think I know what's up."

TRUCE 4: THE FINALE   187

"What is it?" Banks asked.

"Based off of what I heard when you found out what Mason had done, with turning you into a woman for —."

"We all know what he did, nigga." Spacey said, not wanting to remind Banks about that time. Especially since he was partly to blame for deceiving Banks. "Just get to the point."

"All I'm saying is that Shay made a big deal about being the one who knew you weren't dead, Pops. Said nobody believed her and she was by herself."

Spacey looked away. "It's true. She never let it go."

"So, I figure she may be thinking you don't want her around since you never said, well, thank you," Joey continued looking at Banks.

Banks drank the rest of his whiskey and placed his glass down. "I'll be back."

When he left Joey walked up to Spacey, "Is it just me or does Pops seem not to remember me?"

"Why you say that?" Spacey asked, sipping his drink.

"In the boardroom, he recalled everything about ya'll from back in the day but when it came to me, he winked. Fuck was that?"

"Stop being so soft," Spacey said downing all of his drink. "He knows your ass." He bopped out.

Shay almost shitted on herself when she opened the door only to see Banks on the other side. For some reason, she never thought he cared enough to call, let alone show up.

As he stood at the door, with his security detail turned away to look at the streets to be sure no one was approaching, all she could think about was Derrick lying in the basement half dead.

Was he there for him?

"You gonna let me in?" Banks smiled, as he readjusted his shades.

She pulled her soiled robe closed and said, "Sure...uh...sorry." She opened the door wider.

Five minutes later they were drinking coffee in the living room. "Shay, what's going on with you?" He looked her over and it appeared as if she hadn't combed her hair.

She smiled. "Nothing."

His eyes narrowed. "I don't believe you."

She shrugged. "I mean, me and Derrick have been under the weather but for the most part I've been cool. But..."

"I don't know what's going on but understand one thing, I never want you to lie to me. No matter what you have to say I can handle the truth."

She nodded. "I won't lie. Ever."

He sighed. "Now what do you want to ask me? Let it out."

She frowned. "How did you know I wanted to say something to—."

"Shay, what is it?"

She swallowed the lump in her throat. "If something ever happened to me, would you make sure that Patrick is okay? That he would be taken care of?"

He frowned. "Why would you ask me something like that?"

Of course, he would see that he's safe. His name was on the list.

"Because like I said, Derrick and I have been a little under the weather. And I just want to make sure. I promise that's it."

"If something were to ever happen to you, I would raise Patrick like he is my own. That's on my life."

RIVER

River and Tinsley stood in the kitchen as Emo burned fried chicken while also surfing the net at the same time. "...I'm telling you this is right." Emo said as he flipped over a piece of meat so black it would be justice to throw it in the trash as opposed to plopping it on somebody's plate. "This is actually her." He stabbed at his screen with his oily fingertip. "Look at her face. It's the same girl."

Staring at the laptop, River walked slowly backwards until she bumped into the refrigerator. As she took in what was just discovered, Emo walked over to Tinsley and whispered in his ear.

"I see why you like her fine ass," he giggled. "That thing given sexy boy vibes down."

Tinsley pinched him quiet.

To get a better look, River stepped closer to the computer and said, "If this is true and she's—."

"It is true," Emo said cutting River off. "Emo don't make no mistakes when it comes to his research, chile."

"Show me." River said looking up at him.

"Show you what?" The chicken continued to burn causing smoke clouds to hover in the air and all of their clothes to smell like shit.

"Where her people live. If it's true that she was institutionalized at one point, I need to know everything. So, take me."

Later they were knocking at the door of a tiny brickhouse in Richmond Virginia. Within a few minutes an elderly woman opened the door.

"Can I help you all?"

River, Tinsley and Emo shifted a little. After all, she was wearing a white t-shirt that exposed the outline of her flat hanging breasts. And pink boy shorts way too young for a woman of her tenure.

"Can I help you?" She repeated.

River stepped up. "We're sorry to bother you but—.""

"No bother. I haven't had company in over five years." She folded her arms across her chest.

"Well, um, surprise!" Emo said.

Tinsley pinched him quiet again.

"This is getting a little weird." In the background they heard several people who appeared to be mentally challenged. "What do you all want?"

"Do you know a Dasher?" River asked.

Her arms fell at her sides. "You...you know my baby?"

River looked at Emo and Tinsley and back at her. "Yes, can we talk?"

A few minutes later Emo and Tinsley were eating chocolate chip cookies on the sofa. While River sat next to them eager to get down to business. Anita, on the other hand, sat on a rocking chair as she examined each part of their bodies.

Every so often two adults, one a female and the other male in their late twenties would enter and exit, always requiring her attention.

"Excuse the mess, like I said I very rarely have guests." Anita explained.

They looked around and not one single thing was out of place. In fact, the house was so neat it looked as if it were a model home.

"Who are you to Dasher?" River asked.

"I notice you didn't touch any cookies." She pointed at the plate. "They really are very delicious."

"Oh, I'm sorry, I'm not...you know, hungry." She paused. "Now, if you don't mind, I'd like to hear more about Dasher."

"Dasher, is, well, a very special young woman," Anita said as she crossed her arms over her body and squeezed.

"What does that mean?" Tinsley pressed.

"Let the woman talk," Emo said. "Dang."

River looked at him, rolled her eyes and focused back on Anita.

"Dasher, and her siblings," she looked at the adults who played happily with a red ball in the living room, "were born with drugs in their systems."

"What kind?" River frowned.

"Almost every kind imaginable. Crack, heroin, meth. She was very much in the streets and there was no stopping her."

"This is getting good," Emo said rubbing his hands together.

Tinsley glared his way, embarrassed he allowed him to come.

"Well, who is their mother?" River asked.

"My daughter Ann."

River shook her head. "So, basically Dasher is crazy?"

Anita glared. "Be careful, young lady. I invited you in my home out of kindness not to be disrespected."

She looked down, knowing she had more respect than she presented. "Sorry, I just...I mean, I think she may be doing something to my boss."

"Like what?" Anita asked.

"I don't know." River said. "I just got a feeling."

"Should she be worried?" Tinsley added.

"Actually, well, yes."

River's eyes widened. "Why you say that?"

"Dasher showed a propensity for violence unlike her siblings. It presents itself by way of being possessive. She also tends to use her body to rope men. After all, Dasher is a very beautiful woman. But...well...later if things change, her personality shows up as violent if she can't get her way. Now I'm not sure who your friend is, but as long as he's not vulnerable he should be okay."

"Fuck that supposed to mean?" Emo asked.

"Now you being rude?" Tinsley asked.

"It means she's only that way to people who are weaker than her." She paused. "Even in school she had trouble being a bully. So if your friend is not disabled or a baby, he'll be fine."

River's heart thumped and she rose slowly.

"What's wrong?" Tinsley asked.

"I'm not sure but I think Mason's not doing well. When he was in the hospital I called, and I mean I know he was shot but they made me believe that he's paralyzed. I spoke to a nurse there, I think her name is Adrenna. So based on what this lady is saying than that makes him vulnerable. But..."

"What?" Emo said with wide eyes. "Emo's getting scared."

"She also has a baby."

Now Anita rose. "Then I suggest you call the police."

"I...I can't call the police."

"Why?"

"Because…I'm not sure what's in the house."

"Young lady, I don't know what you and your friend are into, but I promise you this, if Dasher is taking care of anybody, it's dangerous."

"What happened to her mother?" Tinsley asked, while River felt as if the room was spinning. "Because my friend needs to speak to her as soon as possible."

"You won't be able to do that. My daughter died in a freak car accident."

"How?" Tinsley pressed.

"While, driving down the street one night, a *bolt* of lightning hit a light pole which fell on the car and killed her instantly."

"Wait…ain't that…"

"The name of her baby," River said interrupting Tinsley. "Bolt."

"My granddaughter has a child?" Anita asked with wide eyes.

"Yeah, she do."

CHAPTER FIFTEEN

WITHOUT PERMISSION

Ace sat on the edge of his bed eating fruit. Although food was provided, his diet at home was healthy and so he wasn't conditioned for processed meals. There was one problem, eating in his room was against the rules.

But he didn't care.

When his doctor walked inside, she was shocked to see the disdain the little boy possessed.

"Ace?"

"Yes?" He bit down into the orange, causing juice to drip down on his chin and the chain he collected yesterday. "Can I help you?"

"Why are you eating in your room?"

"Why do you think?" He shrugged.

She lowered her brow. "I'm an adult."

"I know."

"So be respectful and answer my question."

"Dr. Holman, do you think its dumb to ask questions you already know the answer to?"

She shivered at his level of disrespect. "It depends."

"On what?"

"On the situation." She walked deeper inside. "For instance, you shouldn't be eating in your room. I know you shouldn't be eating in your room and you know this too. And yet here you are, breaking the rules."

"I'm hungry. And I'm not accustomed to being hungry."

"Accustomed?"

He smiled at his use of such a large word. The child loved the dictionary.

"Ace, I'm here because a little boy said you stole his chain."

"I didn't steal anything."

"So that's not his chain on your neck?"

"It is." He bit into the fruit again.

"So, if you didn't steal the chain, why do you have it on?"

Ace stuffed the rest of the fruit into his mouth, wiped his lips with the back of his hand and hopped off the bed. Walking over to his desk, he grabbed a children's dictionary and sat down.

The doctor was stuck and intrigued at the same time. She knew rich children had a way about themselves. But Ace seemed to be in possession of a healthy dose of arrogance and narcissism at the same damn time.

"Okay, this is the definition of steal." He cleared his throat, "*to take without permission.*" He looked at her.

"And?" She shrugged.

"I didn't take it without permission. He gave it to my friend who gave it to me. If anybody should be in trouble it should be my friend."

"Ace."

"I saw you have cameras like I do at home. In the lunchroom."

"Why would you even bring that up?"

"That's how I got here. They caught me on camera with a knife. Look at them. You'll see what I'm saying is true."

"When you get older, you'll discover that you won't be able to do everything you choose, just because you're from a wealthy family."

Ace laughed.

"What's funny?" She asked.

"You know that's not true." He said smiling. "Can I finish eating now?"

Things were falling in line, based on the padfolio in Banks' hands that he played close. He ensured the jet was ready to fly and that his offshore banking accounts were as plump as Georgia peaches.

Now he had to make sure everyone remained safe, and that Ace would be home without a problem. This was proving to be a little more difficult than he originally planned.

He was walking to his Benz when suddenly his phone rang. He started not to answer until he realized it was Tinsley's number. He was the first person who supported him fully after learning that Mason lied to him, and as a result, he always had a place in Banks' heart.

To the point where he extended an invitation for the island that he had yet to accept.

"What's up, Tinsley? How have you—."

"It's River."

He stopped and glared. Jaw twitching, he asked, "Is Tinsley okay?"

"Yes."

"Then why do you have his fucking phone?"

"Please give me one minute."

"You got thirty seconds."

"Okay…I went to Dasher's mother's house. Well actually she was the grandmother and—."

"Fifteen seconds."

"I just found out Dasher is crazy! And she's known for hurting people in fucked up situations. Please, Banks, I need you to check on Mason. I would do it myself but if I'm wrong, the last thing I need is Mason mad at me when this is all said and done."

"What I tell you about contacting me about him?"

"I understand, but I figured now you may feel differently. I'm not talking about wishful thinking. I'm actually talking about she's crazy! Doesn't that change things a little bit?"

"The only thing that's changed is that I want nothing else to do with that nigga. Hit me again and you'll see what I'm capable of. Am I understood?"

Silence.

"Am I clear?" He asked through clenched teeth.

"Yeah, you clear alright."

She ended the call.

For a second Banks stood where he was and looked up at the icy blue sky. Dragging a hand down his face he walked to his car and pulled off.

MINNIE

Minnesota sat in her doctor's office as he looked at the ultrasound machine to be sure the baby was fine. Ever since the bleeding episode, Minnesota had been uneasy and as a result, demanded another appointment.

As the probe glided over her belly due to lots of gel, Dr. Jaric looked at the monitor diligently. "Just as I thought, everything is in order."

Minnesota exhaled and smiled. "Are you sure?"

He flipped the machine off. "Yes I'm sure. But you can't continue to be mobile. I told you we could have sent someone to the house and — ."

"But your assistant said they couldn't do a sonogram there until next week. And my nerves would be bad if I had to wait so long."

"Ms. Wales, I don't want to mislead you. You have a high-risk pregnancy. And it's so important that you follow my instructions. Do not leave your house until after you've had this baby. Now what are you going to do about a nurse?"

"The baby's father is getting one for me."

"Good, because you have to stay in the bed."

"It's going to be hard to — ."

"I've given you my professional opinion, what you do next is up to you." He nodded and walked out.

The moment she pushed the door open to leave the office, the cool night air slapped her in the face. She wasn't going to go so late, but the bleeding made her uneasy. And yet, the moment she walked into the middle of the parking lot she felt scared.

Something was off.

Suddenly a black Dodge with tinted out windows, sped across from her. Within seconds the back windows rolled down and the barrels of two guns winked at her. They didn't wait.

They bucked.

As the bullets flew in her direction, she dropped to the ground. "Oh my God!" She yelled. "Please don't shoot me! I'm pregnant! I'm fucking pregnant!"

The gunmen didn't care as they continued to buck and buck hard in her direction.

Who were these people?

What did they want from her?

Minnesota's emotions were running wild as they appeared to be moving closer for the kill shot. Quickly she rose and ran toward the doctor's office, just as a black van pulled up and struck the Dodge on the side, sending the shooter spinning like a top.

To Minnesota's surprise and relief her hero was Spacey and two other men.

The back door slid open. "Fuck are you doing out here by yourself?" He jumped out and helped her up. "Are you crazy!" He helped her toward the van, as he kept eyes on the gunmen who were trying to get their bearings together.

"Spacey they almost shot me!" She said trembling. "They almost fucking shot me!"

He helped her inside of the vehicle. "I saw that shit! Let's go." He slammed the door and the van pulled away from the scene.

"What were you doing out here alone?" He yelled at her as she continued to cry. "I thought I fucking told you to stay in the house. I thought the doctor told you to stay in the crib too!"

"I needed to make sure my baby was okay!" She sniffled, rubbed her arms, and rocked on the seat. "I...I couldn't feel...like...I didn't believe the baby was still in me."

He shook his head. "Then you should've let somebody go with you!"

"I know, but...I...I was having issues and—."

"Minnie, I don't know what you got going on, but if niggas shooting at you then something is off. Which is even more reason why you need to be going with us on that jet. This is what the fuck I'm talking about!"

She sniffled and wiped the tears away. "Not now, Spacey."

"I get that but—."

"Please. Let's just drop it for now. Okay?"

"Fuck that! If something would have happened to you, I would be dead, Minnie. Is that what you want? I'm surprised you were even able to get away from Pop's detail. How did you shake security anyway?"

"How did you shake security?"

"I have my own crew. So, he gives me leeway if he knows they're with me. Now answer the questions."

"He didn't have but one person on me tonight."

"Why?" He frowned.

"Because like you said, I was supposed to be staying home." She paused. "So, when the guard went to his truck, I walked out the back door and he thought I was still inside." She wiped tears away. "Please don't tell him. He's going to be so mad. He's going to be sooo mad!" She cried harder as she broke into slight delirium.

Spacey moved closer. "I'm not going to say nothing but when are you telling him what you told me?" He paused. "About you not leaving?"

"I don't know."

"Well, you better get it together. Because as you know he's making plans for all of us. And in a minute, he's going to want us in that safe house. Even heard that he's hiring a nurse for you. Some lady who wants to get away from her family due to her abusive boyfriend. Shit is moving fast, Minnie. You better get ready."

After Spacey dropped off Minnesota he drove to a warehouse district. Parking his car on the side of the street, he slipped out and walked up to three dudes standing next to a banged out black Dodge with tinted windows.

Arman unlocked his door, bumped it with the side of his shoulder and pushed it open. Slamming it shut, it barely stayed on. "Fuck you hit my car for?" He pointed back at it like folks didn't see the damage from across town.

Spacey dug into his back pocket. "I had to make it look good." He pulled out a wad of money. "You aight though."

"I get that shit but it wasn't the, plan!"

"You want the money or not? It's as simple as that."

Arman took the cash, counted it, and shook his head. "I don't know what possessed you to order a fake hit on your kid sister, but I hope it's worth it. Because I would've never been able to do that shit if it was me."

Spacey glared. "But it's not you though."

"I'm just saying."

He picked Arman because of his sharp shooting skills but he could do without the condescending attitude. There was something about the way he made his statement that sat wrong in Spacey's soul.

"I can trust you right?" He asked through narrow eyes. "Because I'm not feeling too good about this shit right now."

Arman looked up at him. "Yeah...why you...why —
"

"Can I trust you or not, nigga?"

"Yeah, man!"

"Good, then it's your job to remind me of how much every day of your fucking life. Because if I even think that this shit is coming back on me, I'll find you." He pointed in his chest. "Believe that."

Minnesota was an emotional wreck.

She drew so many conclusions on who could have wanted her dead that she lost count. Had it been years ago, before Banks' surgery, the person could have been anybody. But she was sure she had the deets on who was responsible.

Walking around her bedroom with the cell phone pressed against her ear, she paused when Zercy answered the phone. "So, your family is trying to kill me now? Is that what the fuck is going on?"

"What you talking about?"

"Somebody shot at me tonight, Zercy! While I was at the doctor's office making sure your baby was safe. And as far as I know the only enemies, I have are your siblings. What the fuck is going on over there?"

"Shot at? Oh my God! Are you okay? I'm on my way!"

"Don't come over here! I don't know what my brother may do if he sees you at my house. Just get them bitches together before one of them ends up dead!"

She hung up and stomped toward her bed. Her emotions were all over the place, so when the phone rang again, she answered with an attitude. "Fuck you want?"

"Minnesota, why did you shake Jeff?" Banks asked calmly.

Her eyes widened. "Dad, I—."

"In a matter of days we won't be here anymore. The last thing I need is something happening to you."

"I'm sorry, dad but I swear I am fine."

"When people know you want out, like we do, they want to shut the door on plans. You do know that right?"

"Yes, but I really think I'm safe," she lied.

"That's not good enough for me. I'm bumping up security and I'm hiring a nurse to be with you until we leave. The night before we fly out, I want everyone in the safe house."

"But I—."

"It's settled." He hung up.

She tossed the phone on the bed and yelled, "Fuck!"

CHAPTER SIXTEEN

BURIAL GROUNDS

Jersey picked over her salad in the bowl and pushed it aside when her stomach kept churning. The last thing she wanted was to eat. She needed her life back to normal and since she was on the run for shooting Mason and she hadn't heard from Derrick, she was getting frustrated.

Picking up her cell she made a call.

It was someone she didn't have a relationship with, but at the same time could talk to when things were okay. "Minnie, how are you?"

"Jersey?"

"Yes." She walked to the window and looked at the beach. "It's me. What are you doing?"

"What...what are you doing calling me?" She snapped.

"I wanted to know if, well, how are you first off? I don't want to get straight to the point you know?" She laughed.

Minnesota sighed. "You know it's weird that you're reaching out. To be honest it's not like we ever talked in the first place. So, if you don't mind, I prefer for you to get straight to the point. All I want is to focus on this pregnancy and—."

"Wait, you're having a baby?"

She sighed. "I didn't mean for that to come out."

"That's great news! How are things going?"

"Not good. I've been bleeding and—."

"I bled for the entire pregnancy when I had Howard. Trust me, you'll be fine. Just do whatever the doctor tells you and try your best to take it easy."

"Really? You...you had complications?"

"Yes." She nodded. "And what I want you to know that out of everything I had to deal with, it was stress that sent me over the top. The baby knows when there are issues with the mother. So be sure to take care of yourself."

"Thank you. I...I gotta go. I'm supposed to be—."

"I know. I know. I just wanted to hear your voice and ask if you've heard from Derrick? Or Mason?"

"No, why should I?"

"I haven't been able to reach anybody, Minnesota. Not even Shay. Have you spoken to her at least?"

It wasn't until that time that Minnesota realized she hadn't spoken to Shay in weeks. She was too stressed to focus on anybody but her baby. "No, I'm, I'm sure things are fine though."

"Okay. Well...thank you."

After ending the call with Minnesota, she called Derrick again. Still, she was unsuccessful.

She even hit Mason. She hadn't attempted to reach out to him since she shot him but was so desperate to talk to her son that she took the chance.

Still, she got nothing.

She dialed one final number.

"What I tell you about calling?"

"You have to listen to me, Banks."

"I ain't got to do shit."

She swallowed the lump in her throat and took a deep breath. "If you don't go to the house and see about my son, I'm going to call that facility and tell them about all the shit you and Mason were into back in the day. I'm talking about the drugs, the money and the bodies, Banks. I know everything. I even know burial grounds."

The moment the words left her lips she felt sick to the stomach. And yet her threats were real.

"Banks?"

"Yes."

"Are you going to do it or not?"

"I'll check on him."

"I didn't mean to come at you like that. It's just that I really need to know what's going on. So, thank you for..."

She noticed the dead silence and realized he hung up.

And in that moment, she was in fear for her life.

SHAY

Shay moped into the bathroom preparing to take a bath. Earlier she fed Derrick a basic dinner which included a sandwich and chips. He didn't eat much but she didn't care, because if she knew where he was, which was the basement, it was good enough for her.

DING DONG.

She froze in place.

Her eyes widened.

DING DONG.

Running to the security cameras she was shocked to see Banks and three other men on the other side. What was even more shocking was before she could open the door, Banks had let himself inside of her house.

How did he have the key?

To prevent him from going throughout the home, Shay rushed up to him in the foyer. "Pops, what are you…what are you doing here?"

"Find Derrick and bring him to me," Banks ordered Munro and his men who went through the Louisville Estate without approval.

Shay was so scared she felt woozy.

After his men scattered about, he approached the woman he raised. "Where is Derrick, Shay? And don't lie to me."

"What…I…I mean…."

"Jersey's been calling him. Says she can't reach him. And I wouldn't give a fuck except she trying to get the twins involved now. And I can't have that which you know already. So where is Derrick, Shay? And remember what I said about lying to me."

Her breath rose and fell in her chest. "He's not here." She said holding his arm. "Please, leave."

He stared at her a bit longer. This time through his shades, he sensed danger. He knew when someone committed a crime. That's for sure.

"What did you do?" He stepped closer. "Shay, what happened?"

"He was cheating and —."

"Got him," Munro said carrying a bruised Derrick from downstairs. "He was in the basement."

Banks eyes widened as he peered down at her. "What did you do?"

"He was cheating and I —."

"It doesn't matter," he waved her silent. "I got a lot of shit on my plate and this is the last thing I needed." He looked at Munro. "Take him to the car." He focused back on Shay. "I'll come back for you later. And take a bath. I can smell your pussy from here."

THREE DAYS LATER

Jersey was drop dead gorgeous in a red maxi style dress as she sashayed into the restaurant, she was instructed to meet Banks. The location was at a small town a few miles outside of Virginia Beach.

When she saw the beautiful Mexican restaurant, she originally thought she was in the wrong place, because she didn't know Banks to ever suggest a Latin food establishment.

Walking up to the hostess she smiled. "Hi, I'm here to meet someone." She looked around and saw that not one single person was in the restaurant.

"Sure, what is your name?"

"Why isn't anyone here?" Jersey questioned.

"It's been rented out for the evening. What is your name?"

"Mrs. Wales."

She nodded, grabbed three menus and said, "Follow me."

A second later she was sitting at a booth, in the back that was set for three. The fact that within less than five minutes she would be seeing Banks made her anxious.

Nervous, she swallowed the lump in her throat as she scanned one of the menus. She wasn't even hungry and at the same time, she felt she needed something to go with the liquor she was certain she would be quaffing down her throat.

"Ma..."

Closing the menu slowly, she turned around to see Derrick and Banks standing behind her. He was being supported by Munro and he looked in a bad way.

Slowly she eased out of the booth and wrapped her arms around Derrick. She didn't want to let him go. It had been so long, and his heartbeat told her he missed her too.

"Ma, ma…easy."

She released him and looked at him as he leaned to the side. "What's wrong?" She looked at Banks. "What did you do to my son?"

Silence.

Derrick took a seat and she sat next to him.

"What happened, Derrick?"

"I'm…I'm hurt. But I'll be fine."

Banks sat in front of them while his men remained posted in all corners of the restaurant. Jersey didn't turn to look at all of them, but she could feel their presence.

They were lurking that's for sure.

"You must be a scared man to roll with so much security."

"Scared?" Banks adjusted his shades. "Nah. But when you're protected you can think three steps ahead of everyone else."

She sighed. "Banks, thank you for bringing him to me."

Silence.

She cleared her throat and looked at Derrick. "So where were you? How come you didn't answer my calls?"

"Ma, I'll tell you about it later." He looked at Banks and back at her. It was obvious he wanted away from Mr. Wales as soon as possible.

She nodded and focused on Banks too. His eyes were covered behind shades, but his energy was sinister.

"I wanted you to see your son," Banks said plainly.

"I appreciate that."

"But the threat you leveled against me was serious. You should not have done that. Especially considering our history. You know what I'm capable of, Jersey. What's wrong with you?"

"Oh, Banks, I was just mad and — ."

"How do I know if I were to let you go, that you wouldn't do something to stop me from getting my son? Convince me. I'm listening."

"Ma, what you do?" Derrick asked with a raised brow fully prepared to throw her ass under the bus.

"Nothing, honey." She rubbed his hand.

"Jersey, how do I know?" Banks asked more firmly as a pitcher of sangria was brought to the table.

"Banks, there is nothing in me that wants to see you away from your boys. I carried them in my body for nine months. You know that. I fucking love them too!"

"You haven't answered the question."

"It's just that you wouldn't talk to me. I couldn't find Derrick and I still don't know what's going on with Mason."

"Me either, ma."

"You shot Mason." Banks said. "I could be wrong but that means he's not required to talk to you about shit."

She looked away.

"And again, you haven't answered my question," Banks continued. "How do I know I can trust you, Jersey?"

She started to beg him to let it go but looking at him and how he appeared not to have a care in the world boiled her blood. How dare he let her go so easily, after he killed one of her children.

"You are a selfish man," she said under her breath.

Derrick whipped his head so quickly in her direction he almost broke his neck. "Ma, don't! What are you doing?"

"And I will never, ever let you pretend that you owe me less than your life. I was the one who showed you who you really were after Mason tried to convince you that you were Blaire. Had you sucking his dick and everything. You probably liked that shit now that I think about it." She pointed at him. "So, despite what you say, nigga, you should be kissing my feet."

Derrick felt faint with fear.

Banks removed his shades and smiled. "The real you has shown up. It's about time."

"It's the fucking truth. Mason destroyed you. I built you back up. Show a little courtesy when you look my way." She grabbed the pitcher. "Somebody bring me a fucking glass!"

"I think we should leave," Derrick said. "Plus, I have to tell you what happened with me and Shay."

"In a minute, Derrick."

The waitress walked up to the table and poured them all glasses of sangria. Banks was the first to drink, followed by Jersey who swallowed her entire glass and took another.

Derrick, needing a drink from the moment he'd been rescued, swallowed his entire glass too.

"I'll be back." Banks walked away and went to the restroom.

Munro and the others kept a close watch on them.

"Derrick, what happened?" She whispered, her breath smelling of liquor. "Why hadn't you been calling me back? Was it Banks?"

"Nah, Shay was tripping," he whispered while leaning closer. "She hit me over top of my head." He scratched his dick.

"What? Why? That girl worships you!"

"Went through my shit. Found out I was cheating." He paused and looked around. "But I'm telling you I don't have a good feeling 'bout this." He sipped some more of his freshly poured glass. "Maybe we should just bounce."

She looked at his security. "Nah. It's out of our hands. Plus, Banks would hurt us if we made a move now. Trust me."

"Ma, you shouldn't have said what you said to him. You know how he—."

Suddenly his heart stopped as his eyes focused on a painting on the wall. It was the painting Mason created on Skull Island.

"What's wrong?" She asked, following his gaze.

Now she saw the picture too.

It featured Banks and Mason sitting on the steps in Baltimore city, the place they grew up as kids. Mason had a low cut and Banks had pigtails running down his back.

It told a sad story.

Of happy times gone by.

The richness of the blood colors, which was used to highlight the undertones of Mason's brown skin and the reds of Banks' shirt, were vivid and breathtaking.

What was the painting doing there?

What was the connection?

To those who were there, the portrait meant death.

When Jersey saw the painting, she looked at the jug of wine and then her son. She knew now what was happening.

But it was too late.

Slowly Banks returned, wiping the corners of his mouth with a napkin.

"This is your restaurant?" Jersey asked.

"Yes."

"When did you have the painting brought here?"

"When we returned from Skull Island and I bought the place. I heard about it from a customer who lived in the Virginia Beach area. Said he couldn't keep up the payments and I love Mexican food, so it was a perfect fit. I'm giving it back to him now though. Since I'm leaving the country."

Suddenly Jersey felt drowsy, and Derrick was already leaning to the left.

The sangria was the same poisonous mixture that killed Arlyndo.

And now it would take out his mother and brother too.

"How could you do this to me?" Jersey said, as the poison made its way through her body.

"I asked you a simple question. You gave me your answer. And I'm not going to have anything, or anybody come in the way of me and my sons."

"I would never have done what I said, Banks," she cried before looking at Derrick whose eyes were open but lifeless. "Please, it's not too late. Call for hel…"

Her eyes fluttered and it was obvious she was fighting.

Fighting for life.

Fighting for love.

Her neck fell heavily backwards. "Did you…ever…love me?" Her words were but a whisper.

Banks rose and closed Derrick's eyes who had already slipped away. Next, he kissed her lips and whispered in her ear.

"I loved you but you're disloyal. And for that you gotta die." He grabbed his shades, slipped them back on and exited the restaurant.

He didn't give a second thought to either of them when he departed.

The next morning Banks sat on the edge of his bed with the cell phone next to him. When the doorbell rang, he walked slowly toward the foyer. He didn't have to worry about it being someone wanting to do him harm because whoever got past the guards were either on the list or police.

Opening the door, he faced two detectives. Both male and in their late forties.

"Yes." Banks crossed his arms over his chest.

"Are you Mr. Wales?"

"I am."

"We are here to inform you that Jersey Louisville and her son Derrick Louisville were found dead in a motel room outside of Virginia Beach. Jersey had your number in her phone, and we wanted you to know personally."

They waited for a response from Banks. Anything to detect his guilt.

They received nothing.

"It looks like it was a murder suicide, but we'd still like to ask you a few questions if you don't mind."

"I'm actually pretty busy."

"It won't take long, sir."

Banks allowed them inside, but it was all a ruse. He wanted them the fuck up out his crib so he could care for other matters. At the end of the day, they were there for fifteen minutes and he let them talk while he listened. When it was all said and done, it was a complete waste of time.

After they left, he grabbed his cell and made the call. The call that was the entire purpose of the events in the first place.

"In case you haven't heard, Jersey Louisville killed herself." He told Marjorie Holman. "Now you can let my boy go."

"I'll...I'll look into it."

"Look, check, do whatever the fuck you gotta do. Because time is almost up. Free Ace Wales."

When he ended the call, he got another one right after it. He sighed when he saw the caller's name on the ID.

"Banks, you might as well change your number because I'm not giving up." River sounded like she was on the verge of tears but was holding back. If nothing else, he knew in that moment Mason chose right by having her in his corner.

"What do you want, River?"

"Mason just lost his son, and I went by to tell Dasher. But she still not letting me inside, and I need to be there for him! Please go see about him. I'm begging. You do this and I'll never bother you again. I swear!"

CHAPTER SEVENTEEN

NAH

The window was open to allow a breeze into the Louisville Estate. Shay sat on the living room sofa with Joey and his wife sitting next to her. To say she was in a bad way was an understatement.

"He's dead..." she whispered. "I...I can't believe he's dead. I...I don't know what I'm going to do now."

Joey moved closer and rubbed her back. "I'm sorry, sis. I know how you felt about him. Ya'll been together forever. And we had our problems, but he was like a brother to me too. I would never want to see him go out like this." He shook his head. "Jersey killing everybody. This shit crazy."

She looked at him. "He's actually dead, Joey."

"I'll go make some tea," his wife said leaving them alone.

"Did he say anything that would let you know this would happen?"

"I found out not to long ago he was cheating on me." She sniffled. "And I...Joey, I lost it. I didn't understand how he could...how he..." her words disappeared as the weight of Derrick being dead pressed on her harder. "And the things I did to him...how I treated him was the last thing he remembered of me."

"You don't have to say anything else."

"He's gone, Joey. Who's going to love me now?"

"What you saying, Shay?!"

"I'm serious!" She cried as huge tears rolled down her face. "I'm all by myself, Joey. And I've never felt this type of loneliness before."

"You got us!"

"I don't!" She yelled. "You have a family. Pops has a family. Minnesota is about to have a baby. And I don't even know what's going on with Mason. Who do I have? Tell me that?"

"What about Patrick? Your son is a direct bloodline to him." He paused. "So never think you are alone."

"I won't make it after this, Joey." She shook her head slowly from left to right. "I'm telling you."

"Here's the tea," Sidney said as she reentered the room. "I bought cream, milk and sugar because I didn't know if you wanted anything else with it."

Shay stood up. "I'll be back." She walked out with her head low.

Joey's wife sat next to him. "She looks bad. Like really, bad. And I've seen this kind of thing before."

"I know, man. Me too."

"Maybe we should stay with her."

He looked at her for a second and smiled. "You know I appreciate this right? You stepping up and all."

"I'm your wife. And this is your family. Whatever you need I'm here for." She kissed his lips. "There's no reason to thank me."

He nodded. "I do think we should stay the night but I'm also thinking we should get somebody to stay with her until we fly to the island."

She looked away.

"What?"

"Nothing...uh...I mean...I think she may need professional help too. I've seen that look before when working with people who can't get past the damage they did while using drugs. And having somebody look at her versus look after her is two different things all together."

He nodded. "So, what do you think we should do?"

"Maybe get the police involved."

He frowned and waved the air. "Nah."

"Nah? Even if it means saving her?"

"Bae, we aren't the police type of family."

"I'm not understanding what that means."

"Just what I said. When we have problems, we throw money on it and take care of it ourselves."

"What is it about this family?"

"Meaning?"

"Why does there seem to be an air of secrecy around you guys at all times? I'm telling you that she—."

THUMP. THUMP.

"What the fuck was that?" Joey said running toward the sound.

It took a while but before long they found the source. It came from the kitchen. When Joey bent the corner, he saw Shay lying on the floor with both of her wrists slit open.

DASHER

Trash bags lined the walls within Dasher's home as she sat in the dining room eating stuffed shrimp. Bolt was in his highchair while Mason was in his wheelchair with so many bruises on his face it was hard to recognize him.

If it was meant to be exact, it was accurate to say she was abusive.

Life had hit him in more ways than one.

After all, in addition to being beaten daily, he learned from Dasher not even a few minutes earlier, that his ex-wife and son had participated in a murder suicide.

And just that quickly his original bloodline was gone.

Now, all he had in the world was Ace, Walid, Bolt and his grandson Patrick and he was certain based on the way things were going that he would never see them again.

"Don't look so sad, Mason," She said as she cut into her food. "You still got me. If you ask me, it's a good fucking day."

In that moment the hate he felt for the woman bubbled to the surface. Yeah, he didn't fuck with Jersey, after all she shot him. But she was still the mother of his deceased children and he still lost his eldest son.

"You will pay for what you doing to me," Mason said plainly. "I hope you know that."

She glared. "Will I?"

Silence.

"Mason, when you act right, that is, treat me right, I will *treat you right* too. Until then, we will continue to have a problem. Because — ."

DING DONG.

Her eyes widened and she dropped the fork on her plate. It plopped to the floor. Quickly she popped up and ran toward Mason. Grabbing his handlebars, she shoved the chair toward the linen closet in the back of the house.

DING DONG. BANG. BANG. BANG.

Opening the door, she dumped him in the closet like trash and pushed away his chair. Walking back up to him she said, "I better not hear shit from you." She pointed a yellow finger in his face. "If I do, you may find yourself one more son short." She slammed the door.

DING DONG. BANG. DING DONG. BANG. BANG. KICK.

Rushing back up to the front door she looked down at her clothes, brushed off a few crumbs and opened it wide. It was Banks and his crew on the other side.

"Go look for Mason," Banks said as his men rushed through the house.

"Hold up! I didn't give you permission to enter my house!"

Banks shoved her to the right and walked inside. "Save us some time and tell us where Mason is in this bitch."

Her eyes were so wide she looked like she would pass out. He was different than River and she knew one wrong move and she would be worse off than she started. "He's not here!" She yelled, hoping the niggas in the back would hear her voice and stop their search.

They didn't.

"This is wrong! You have to leave!"

"Nah, not until I see him for myself."

"Why do you care? Ya'll not even friends anymore."

"Why you keeping him from his people?"

"His people?"

"I'm sick of hearing folks tell me you not letting them see him. If he's fine, let me see him and we'll bounce."

She pointed at him. "Wait, I know what this is about," she smiled, regaining control. "You feel guilty don't you?"

"Fuck are you talking about now?"

"You had something to do with Jersey and Derrick dying?"

Silence.

"Well, if I were you, I'd be at ease." She giggled.

"You don't know what you talking about, bitch." He stepped closer.

She dug in her pocket and pulled out a pink cell phone.

"What you doing?"

"You'll see." She turned it on. "I want to show you something." She scrolled through the screen until she reached text messages. She went to the one with Mason and showed him her phone. "Look."

"Look at what?"

"The messages he sent me in the past. Read them and then tell me if you still feel like saving him."

Banks glared. "What are you, fourteen years old?"

"Okay, I'll read them for you..." She cleared her throat. *"That nigga is a bitch...Fuck the nigga Banks. He thinks he's a dude. He forgot he sucked my dick...couldn't even keep him off it he liked it so much."*

As she went on and on, Banks grew heated.

"We can't find him," one of his men said as the rest of them piled back into the living room.

"See, I told you." Dasher said proudly.

"Let's get out of here." Banks said staring at her, angry about how Mason talked behind his back.

The embarrassment was crippling.

Dasher grinned wider. "Come back any time."

When they walked outside, Banks removed his cell phone from his pocket and dropped it to the ground. Smashing it into a million pieces he resolved in that moment not to take another call from anybody that wasn't related to his plan to go to his island or get Ace out of the home.

And that included River.

Or Mason.

CHAPTER EIGHTEEN

THE FOREWARNING

The nurse Banks hired checked the fluids running into Minnesota's veins as she lie in bed. When she was certain the levels were good, she checked her temperature next. The way she fussed over her drove Minnesota insane, but these things had to be done.

Tossing due to irritation, Minnesota yelled, "That's enough! You been poking and prodding me all damn day!"

The nurse jumped back but was given specific orders to make sure everything Minnesota needed health wise was provided. "I just need to—."

"Please leave me alone."

When the woman looked like she was about to cry, it was then that Minnie saw the fear in her eyes.

"I'm sorry…I just wanted to make sure that you were well. I was told that if something happened to you, something would happen to me too."

Minnesota was shocked at how serious Banks was with the details. "Listen, don't worry. I'll, I'll tell my father that you are doing a wonderful job. And that you made me feel better."

"Really?"

"Yes, but I need you to go and not come back in here unless I ask." She said waving her toward the door. "Okay?"

She nodded rapidly. "Of course." With those words the nurse left her alone.

Taking a deep breath Minnie made a call from her cell. When she heard her brother's voice she smiled, "How is Lila? Did everything go as planned or did she try and fight again?"

"I didn't take him to see her yet."

"Spacey, what are you doing? This is so wrong."

"I know, it's just that, well, I think she should get used to not having him around since she won't after we leave."

"It may seem like it's simple for you, but it won't be for her. Let her be with her son. Don't try to reduce shit to logic. It doesn't work that way."

"It's true. Once we get on that jet it's over. Even though the plan is to send her videos of Riot growing up happily, at the end of the day she won't be in his life."

"Maybe you're right." She paused. "I just can't imagine what she's going to be like when you call her and tell her Riot is gone forever."

"To be honest I don't even care. I got other shit on my mind."

"Like what?"

"About you not coming with us. After that shootout, you can't stay here and expect shit to go smoothly when we leave. You will always have to look over your shoulder. Even if Pops leaves security."

"I'll be fine." She paused. "And I..." When she looked down and saw she received another call on her cell she said, "I have to go. I'll hit you —."

"I'm gone, I'm gone. Just remember to stay in the house, Minnie. If not for yourself, for your baby." He ended the call.

She rolled her eyes.

"Hello."

"You answered," Zercy breathed in relief. "But please don't hang up. I just wanna talk to you right quick."

"About what, Zercy?"

"I want to know how you doing? I want to know how you feeling? And to see if I could do anything. Anything at all."

"I have a chance to get away."

"What does that mean?"

She didn't bother telling him about Banks flying her out of the country forever. Because she was certain that conversation would spark a whole different level of anxiety for him.

And yet she wanted to forewarn him a little.

"It means just what I said. I have a chance to be safe, happy and healthy with my baby. But I want you to be in your child's life. But you must get a hold of your family. Because I can promise you this, there is no way I'll be around only for me and the baby to live in fear."

The wind picked up a bit as Zercy lie face up on the bed trying to think of a way to make things right.

Taking a deep breath, he closed his eyes and said, "God I'm trying to be calm. I'm trying to keep a level head, but I can't lose Minnesota. So, I'm asking that you move all of our enemies out of the way that will stop us from being happy. But if you can't, I need you to forgive me in advance for the moves I make. Amen."

Spacey looked at Lila from the inside of his car while she hugged her son. She lost a considerable amount of weight since she almost died due to Ace putting a marble in her popcorn and later opting to have weight loss surgery.

As he watched them talk and connect, he realized something in that moment.

He hated her.

He hated her for not being strong enough not to let herself go physically.

He hated her for meeting men on the net and allowing them to use her body. And he hated her for not being Minnesota Wales, despite knowing the attraction wasn't right.

When they were done talking, he got out of the car and picked up the little boy. He noticed that she was crying.

"Spacey, something is going on!" She sniffled as she wiped her tears away.

"I'm bringing you your son and all you can do is accuse me?"

"I'm sorry I just...I wish..." She looked at Riot who was intent on staring in his direction. "Just, take care of him. Make sure he's okay and, and tell him how much I love him. Every day."

"You'll be able to tell him your —."

"Spacey, stop lying." She sniffled again. "Just tell him how I feel and, and, and..." she slammed the door crying leaving them alone.

Spacey shrugged, not caring either which way. "You ready, lil' man?"

"Yep! I told mama I'm going to the island." He said excitedly as they hit it back to the car.

"Damn," he said.

That's why she fucked up.

CHAPTER NINETEEN

MIST

Sidney and Joey stood next to Shay's bed. To be honest he hadn't left her side since she attempted suicide. His concern for her was great because in a lot of ways, he saw himself through her when he was at the height of his addiction.

Her eyes were closed but he felt in his heart that she wasn't sleep. And as he looked down at the bandages on her wrists he sighed.

"Shay, I know you can hear me." He said softly. "You don't have to answer, but I wish you would. What are you doing? Why are you hurting yourself? Talk to me. Say something."

She shook her head and slammed her lids tighter together. "Where is Patrick?"

"Morgan has him."

She sighed. "Good. He needs to be as far away from me as possible. Because...because I...I don't want to be here anymore. I don't, I don't feel like I have anything left to live for."

"But this ain't the way."

"Maybe I should leave you two alone," Sidney said walking toward the door.

"No," Shay said opening her eyes. "I need...I need a female presence here right now." She paused. "After all, you're a Wales too." She smiled but it melted away a few seconds afterwards. "Whatever that means."

Sidney wiped her blonde hair from her face and sat in one of the two available chairs in the room. "O...okay."

"Shay, I'm not with this weak shit. I'm not gonna lie."

Looking up at Joey she said, "You don't know what it feels like to be alone. You don't know how it feels to look around and not have anybody to understand you.

I don't want to be here, Joey. I know what I'm saying even if you don't. And I'm praying hard for my release."

"Did you actually say that I don't understand?" Joey said with a hand over his heart. "Me?"

Silence.

"Have you forgotten that I had to fight my way out of an addiction? That I tried to kill myself with drugs and was almost successful until Pops caught me and put me in that makeshift rehab? And that even then I would've died until I found my wife? If anybody understands you its me."

"That's just it!" Shay said louder. "You found someone!"

"And you will too!" He yelled. "But this ain't the way, Shay. Plus doing this right now would destroy my father and I can't have that. He's been through too much to have one of his kids tap out now."

"He doesn't give a fuck about me."

"If you really believe that, why won't you let me tell him you're here? Why won't you let me tell anybody?"

She closed her eyes again as more tears poured down her cheeks.

"I'm begging you not to give up. You saved my father before when you didn't give up and forced niggas to remember his name. You'll save him again by staying alive. Come with us to the island. Sit on sand, eat, do and be whatever you want for every day you breathe. And if you still want to take your life, I won't stop you. I may even help."

MINNESOTA

DAYS LATER

Minnesota was feeling better, and she was tired of being in the house. And so, she sat at a park, on a bench after having agreed to meet Zercy alone.

When he finally pulled up in a new black pickup truck she rose. Quickly he exited the vehicle and walked toward her. Slowly at first and then quicker until they were face to face.

Grabbing her up softly by the arms, he looked her over. His anxiousness falling on her like mist from the sky begging to rain. "How are you? Are you hurt? Do you need anything?"

"No, I'm fine."

"I really wish you let me come see you. I thought you weren't supposed to be out of bed? Won't you —."

"I'm here, Zercy. You wanted to see me, and I snuck out of the house and away from security. Besides, like I said I needed fresh air. I'm tired of being looked over like the president's daughter."

He chuckled once. "How did you even escape?"

She laughed. "Shaking security ain't new to me. I been sneaking away from the details my father placed on me since I was a little girl. As a matter of fact, whenever we moved to a new house, the first thing I would do is learn the escape routes."

He shook his head and softly pulled her down to sit on the bench. "I still think you need to be in the house, but this won't take long."

"It's okay. We're safe. As long as I get home before the next shift, we're good."

He shook his head. "I wanted to see you because I think we will be fine now." He placed a hand on her belly. "In fact, I'm sure."

She frowned. "Whatever, Zercy."

"Give me a chance to explain. Please."

"I'm sorry. The nurses and the security coupled with my hormones have been driving me crazy. I barely get sleep which is why I wanted to leave the house tonight. For some air. I feel like I'm locked up."

He nodded. "That makes me feel better because I want nothing more than for you and my baby to be safe."

"So, what is your plan for them? Because Zercy, I think things will get worse first. Whatever weird family dynamic you got going on is spilling over towards me."

He nodded and exhaled. "You're right. But we —."

Suddenly, the triplets stepped out of the bushes. Their expressions were flat, and they looked as if they had nothing but malice toward both of them.

"Fuck are ya'll doing here!" Zercy yelled. "What's...what's going on?"

"So, I was raped, and you didn't even care?" Ziamond asked. "You didn't even call to see if I was okay."

"I didn't call because I didn't believe you."

She laughed. "You right, I was lying. I just wanted to see if you had any love left for us before we did whatever we needed to do next."

"What does that mean?"

"I guess you're about to find out, big brother."

Suddenly a truck drove through the grass and up to them at a quick rate. Zercy, in protection mode, immediately stood in front of Minnesota. When the doors popped open, and he saw masked men his heart dropped.

"What the fuck is going on?" He looked at his sisters. "What are you doing? Tell me now!"

"Zercy," Minnesota trembled. "What's happening?"

"Nobody is going to hurt you!" He said over his shoulder at her before focusing back on them. "Now I don't know what ya'll got planned, but if you do this we are done. Forever! I'm telling you right now that this is the line in the sand!"

"She's coming with us, big brother," Ziamond grinned. "I just wanted to be a woman and tell you upfront. Instead of snatching her off the streets."

But Zercy hadn't been right since he learned Minnesota was almost killed. And so, he whipped out a handgun he had tucked in his waist.

Everyone, even the men in the truck paused.

"Call them off, Ziamond!" He warned aiming wildly. "Now!"

"You're pulling a fucking gun out on her?" Zuri asked. "Your own sister."

"Have you lost your mind?" Ziggy yelled.

"Tell them to get the fuck out of here!" He cocked and maintained his aim at Ziamond. "If they move, I will shoot you first. I'm not fucking around!"

She laughed and took one more step. "You actually think I believe you would—."

Immediately, he shot at the bench, but the bullet ricocheted and hit Ziamond. With her chest opening causing blood to spill, she dropped to the ground and his eyes widened in shock.

Realizing what he did, he rushed toward her and grabbed her up. "Fuck! Why did you make me do this?"

"You shot her!" Zuri cried. "You fucking shot your own sister!"

Seeing the melee, and with Zercy's guard down, the men charged Minnesota. When Zercy saw this, he released Ziamond and went to help but one of the men stole Zercy in the face while the other two grabbed Minnesota and took her to the truck.

Within seconds, she was kidnapped.

And he was out cold.

THE HOSPITAL

The room where Zercy's sisters were sitting waiting for the news of Ziamond's fate was packed. In fact, so many people were present that some had to wait out in the parking lot. And it was there that Zercy sat in his truck to see if he actually killed his own sibling.

When he saw his last two remaining sisters rushing out of the hospital crying, he had gotten his answer.

Gripping the steering wheel, he cried quietly. This was not what he wanted. And yet he felt like it was the accumulation of so many events that it all made sense. The obsession they had for him.

Their need to not want other people in his life.

All brought the events in question.

In an accident, nothing more than a ruse meant to prevent Minnesota from getting hurt, he murdered his sibling.

Slowly he pulled away from the scene on what would be described as one of the worst days of his life.

Because there was still a major question in play.

Where was Minnesota Wales?

Minnesota sat in the back of the truck with a sack over her head.

She couldn't believe how not listening to her father resulted in her being kidnapped and possibly killed or raped.

What was to happen to her baby? She touched her growing belly in fear.

What was to happen with her life?

Why couldn't she follow the rules? It was as if Minnesota got off on drama and used every opportunity to wreak havoc. Whether she knew it or not.

When the truck finally stopped, she felt her bladder about to release. "Please don't hurt me." She sobbed. "I'm, I'm rich and if you give me a chance, I can get some money. I can call my father and he'll bring over stacks. I promise."

Silence.

Just the activity of people entering and leaving the truck put her on edge. When she heard someone approaching, her heart thumped harder.

She decided to talk louder. Maybe they didn't understand that with one call, she could make them wealthy for life. "Did you hear me? I can get you the—."

When the sack was snatched off her head, she was about to scream until she saw her father standing in front of the men who took her moments earlier. They were in a warehouse district.

Banks had so many men behind him it looked like they were guarding the President of the United States.

"What's going on?" Minnesota asked huffing and puffing.

"I thought I told you to stay in the house?"

"But I, I—."

"You almost got yourself killed." He stepped closer.

"What's going on, Dad?" She looked at him and then the strangers.

"Don't you realize there's nothing I'm not willing to do to keep you safe?"

"You said you would never do this again!" She cried. "And you broke your promise!"

He frowned having no memory of such a promise. "What are you talking about?"

"This isn't the first time you had me kidnapped, dad. What if someone would've hurt me? How did you know you could trust your men who took me?"

"These aren't my men. And I trust people to move how they are by nature." He paused. "Which is why I have a retainer for the streets. That if anybody were to attempt to take a Wales member, I would double the price if you were returned." He paused. "Now get out. You're going to the safe house. I'm keeping my eyes on—."

"I'm not going, Dad."

He frowned. "What you talking about?"

"I can't leave with you to the island. I'm sorry but I can't. I—."

"Minnesota, if you stay here you will die. With every passing day you create more enemies. Now I can't force you to go to the island. You're a grown woman. But I won't be able to protect you if you don't let me. Is this what you want? To live in constant fear?"

Banks' phone rung and he quickly answered. "What is it, Joey? It's a bad—."

"It's about Shay."

He stepped away from the truck. "What about her?"

"Something happened a few days back. And I'm sorry I'm just telling you now."

"Well, what happened?"

"She tried to take her life."

"Where is she now?"

"Back at the Louisville Estate."

"I'm on my way."

He hung up and looked at Munro. "Get her to the safe house." He looked at his security. "Everybody cover it to make sure she's safe."

"What about them?" Munro asked looking at the men who betrayed their boss to get the bag.

"Pay 'em." He quickly got in his car and winked at Munro.

That meant they would be dead within the hour.

Banks rushed into the Louisville Estate where Shay was sitting in the living room on a chair. Dark shades covered his eyes because lately any kind of light caused his headaches to get worse.

When he saw her, he almost couldn't believe his eyes. She lost so much weight and was wearing bandages over both wrists and a hospital band on her left arm.

He looked around. The house was a mess. "Shay, where is Patrick? Is he okay?"

"At Ms. Morgan's house." She paused. "How come you gave everybody security but me? If you had, you would've known what I went through. You would've known I went to the hospital. You would've known it all. But you didn't because after all this time, you still don't consider me a Wales."

He shifted a little.

He did care but he didn't provide her security primarily because he thought no one in the streets would snatch her because she didn't bare his last name.

It was a bad look on his part, considering she was on the list.

"I was wrong. But what are you doing?" He asked in a heavy tone. "Joey said you hurt yourself. Why would you do this?"

She looked up at him and he could feel all the pain she was in at that moment. "Is this about Derrick?"

"How do you get out of darkness when you can't see the light?" She said in a low voice. "How do you feel better when you are too weak to even try?"

Banks thought about what he'd gone through. "You get mad. Real mad. It's the next step up before change. Now what's going on with you?"

"I lost everyone. My mother. My father. Harris. Derrick and even you."

He sighed and grabbed a chair to sit directly in front of her. "Shay, listen to me. I know you may feel like nobody loves you. And I'm sorry I haven't been able to show you in the way you need. But I promise you, if you come with me to this island, you will see what you mean to me." He touched the side of her face. "Do you hear me? I want you there with me. At my side."

Although dark shades with a slight reflection covered his eyes, she believed him. Before that moment she wasn't clear on how he felt about her. She wasn't even certain if he liked her.

All her doubts were wiped away. "You do care about me?"

"Shay, I consider you a daughter. And I never got to say thank you for not giving up on me. For keeping me in the minds of people who thought I was dead. Thank you for that because it was loyalty at the highest level." He readjusted. "And I'm sorry about Derrick too. I know what he meant to you."

She sniffled. "Why are you sorry?"

He had his reasons but kept them to himself. "Because, because I know what he meant to you. Even with everything that..."

Suddenly her eyes widened as she stared at him intensely.

"What's wrong?" Banks asked.

In a flash, Shay jumped up and covered Banks with a weird hug that surrounded his upper body and head, just as a bullet came from the window and ripped through Shay's back.

A bullet that was intended for Banks.

Had she not seen the gunman's reflection through his shades, he would be dead.

Blood splattered everywhere as her limp body hung in his arms. "Shay!" He yelled. "Shay!"

Grabbing his cell phone out of his pocket he made a call. "Get over to the Louisville Estate! Now!"

Having kept all his security with Minnesota, he left himself exposed.

It was a major slip up on his part. But when it came to his children, he often held a blind spot. Which is why he wanted them all safe.

He tossed his phone down and held Shay in his arms as she took her last breath.

CHAPTER TWENTY

BREAKING GLASS

Zantonio was pacing the living room in his mansion with rage. After all he just learned that one of his three sisters died by the hands of their brother. Zuri and Ziggy were with him, both still rattled at the loss of a family member.

"What are we going to do?" Zuri yelled. "Because you better not ask me to forgive him. He killed her! He fucking killed her! I was there!"

"Why would you go to the Louisville Estate to kill Banks?" He was panicking and the pitch of his voice was as high as a woman's. "Let's talk about that. And more than anything why would you miss? Do you realize how much shit you just brought on us? What if he saw you? And then ya'll come here!"

"Oh, so now you scared. Because guess what, I'm going for our dear old brother next."

"I thought you said…I thought you said when he killed Ziamond it was an accident."

"I don't give a fuck what it was! You don't point your gun at a family member. You don't—."

Suddenly, Zercy walked inside. He raised the key Zantonio had given him years ago. "I'm glad we're all together." He tossed the key on the floor. "Won't be needing that shit no more."

Zuri rushed up to him. "You're a fucking traitor!" She spit at his feet.

He walked around the creamy glob and toward Z's bar. "We have to talk." He poured himself a glass of Hennessey. "Now."

"About what?" Z asked.

"I been thinking." He took a sip. "And I finally get what all of this has been about. All the obsession with the sisters. All of the playing me close."

"What you talking about, nigga?" Zantonio asked.

"What happened the day ma and dad died?" He drank everything in his cup and sat at the dining room table. "Tell me the truth. No more lies. No more beating around the bush."

Zuri and Ziggy looked at Z who sighed.

"You know what happened." Z said. "You got some of the insurance money too. Or do you wanna fake like you innocent?"

Zercy shook his head slowly from left to right.

"You know what, I'm tired of playing this game. Yes, we killed them," Zuri said.

"What are you doing?" Zantonio yelled glaring her way.

"Finally bringing closure to this shit!" She walked up to the table. "Why should we protect him when he don't give a fuck about us?" She looked at Zercy. "We killed them because they locked us in our rooms, treated us like shit and didn't give a fuck if we lived or died.

And when we talked about killing them you were in the building that night too. So don't fake. You helped us go over details."

"We were fucking kids! We were just talking! Like kids do when they can't get their way with their parents!"

"Lies!" Ziggy said.

"Facts!" Zercy made the correction. "And you knew I wanted no part of it because you tried to kill me too. When that house blew up with mom and dad in it, I was there. Had it not been for me walking to the car to get their gift, I would not be here. All of you were gone and you wanted me dead because I wasn't with the plan. And then you killed my girlfriend because you thought I told her. That's probably why you want Minnesota dead too. Right?"

He looked at all three.

Their silence gave him his answer.

"You have ruined my life and the only reason you killed everybody close to me is because you know there is no statute of limitations on murder."

"You killed our sister!" Zuri redirected.

"And I'll spend the rest of my life feeling guilty about that shit too." He pointed. "But let's be clear, you all wanted me dead long ago. And what you're doing now is wrong. Minnesota don't have shit to do—."

"I don't want to talk about that bitch!!" Zuri yelled. "I want to talk about your loyalty!"

"I *am* talking about loyalty!" He yelled standing up before slamming his fist into the table. "What's more loyal than making sure the mother of your future child is safe?" He paused. "Where is she?" He looked at the trio. "Where is Minnie?"

Zantonio looked away.

"Where is Minnesota?" Zercy repeated again.

"I don't have her."

"I saw your men take her away, Z. I saw them. So, tell me where she is or else there will be a problem."

"Or what you gonna do? Kill us too, big brother?" Ziggy cried.

"Please, man, she has my—."

"I don't know where she is, Zercy." Zantonio interrupted. "And that's the honest truth. If I knew I would get her myself because she's a Wales. And right now, the Wales' are worth millions."

He frowned. "Wait, you hired outsiders to do an important job again?"

Zantonio glared. "I just told the streets to seek and find. What they did with that information is above me now."

"That's why you ain't got no business being a bad guy, Z," he shook his head. "That's why the pussy business you in dried up. Because you not built for this shit."

"Be easy, twin."

"Nah, you be easy." He shook his head slowly. "Because you just declared war on the richest nigga in the world. And you aren't prepared by taking his daughter."

Suddenly, Ziggy, broke one of the liquor bottles on the bar and charged toward Zercy. She almost hit him until he knocked her down with a fist to the center of the face, just as five men rushed into the side doors.

Glass breaking everywhere.

"PUT YOUR FUCKING HANDS IN THE AIR!" One of them yelled. "NOW! IT'S NOT A FUCKING GAME!"

Everyone obeyed and quickly threw their hands up as the men took both twins and rushed out of the house.

Zercy pulled up to Banks' mansion. After the car was checked for weapons, he was immediately allowed on the property. Once inside, he was led to the lounge where Banks was waiting on him.

He was sitting calmly in his recliner, smoking a cigar. Shades still in place.

"Sit down."

Zercy stepped deeper inside. "I appreciate you meeting with—."

"Sit down."

Slowly Zercy took his seat across from him. "I hate that we're officially meeting like this, Mr. Wales. But I want you to know—."

"Minnesota is safe." Banks said pulling off his cigar. "But I guess you figured it out which is why you're here."

"Yes." It still felt good to hear.

"How did you know?"

"When we first got together, she said you were smart. That you always had a plan that was miles ahead of what other people did. And when I saw them come into my brother's house, I realized I also saw one of the men watching over Minnie's house in the past."

"Very perceptive." Banks nodded. "What do you want?"

"My sisters. Where are they?"

Banks stood up and hit the bar. "You smell like you been drinking cheap shit. You want a glass of richness?"

He nodded and Banks poured two glasses of expensive whiskey. Keeping one for himself. "Drink up. Every drop."

"Why?"

"You're going to need it after what I tell you next."

Zercy drank it all and swallowed the growing lump in his throat. "Okay, I'm ready."

Banks picked up the phone and called his man inside. When Munro entered, he held an iPad in his hand.

"Earlier tonight I went to see about Shay. She's like a daughter to me."

"I'm aware."

Suddenly Banks' energy grew darker. "Well, are you also aware that she gave her life for me? Because one of your sisters, I can't tell the difference between the two, shot at me in her house?"

Zercy's eyes widened. "No, they, they wouldn't have done—."

"I gave you a drink. Don't insult me in my home by calling me a liar."

Zercy looked down. "You have to understand, we grew up in a tough environment where—."

"Fuck that shit!" He yelled waving the air. "I'm from BALTIMORE CITY! Everybody got a fucking sob story! You don't know what it's like to grow up in hell unless from the day you were able to remember, you felt like you were in a body not your own. You don't know what it feels like to lose children and everybody else around you too. Just because you're wealthy." He pointed behind him. "Them bitches shot at me and I can't let that ride!"

"Banks, please don't —."

"Show him."

The man showed Zercy a video of his sisters lying on a basement floor in puddles of their own blood. It looked violent as splatters were even on the walls. Holes on every part of their bodies.

Zercy dropped to his knees and vomited.

"Like I said, I couldn't tell the difference between the two. So, I took them both." He took a sip. "Your brother is next."

"Why? I don't understand?"

"He put a hit on me and my family. It was discovered tonight. And I can't have that."

Zercy wanted to throw up more. "Why…why is there so much blood?"

"Let's just say they didn't make things easy. They were fighters. But I guess you know that already."

"Why, Mr. Wales?" Zercy cried. "Why kill them both?"

"I told you already! They look identical. And because I'm told my daughter, my flesh and blood, wants to stay here when I made plans for her elsewhere. And if she stays, I can't be concerned about her well-being. I'll empty out this whole state before I leave her behind while she's under attack. So, your brother is — ."

"Don't, do anything to my brother yet." He said with raised palms. "Please."

Banks readjusted. "Why should I wait?"

"I just want five minutes with him first, sir."

"I'll give you two. And if I even think you are trying to alert him about my next move, I'll force that baby out of Minnesota and gut you next."

CHAPTER TWENTY-ONE

WIPED OUT

B anks sat in Dr. Holman's office, within the facility, preparing to take Ace home. But the moment he saw her face he knew once again that things would not go as planned.

Because of her inability to bend, he had yet to take this item off his list.

"How are you, Mr. Wales?" She walked in wearing a tight red dress and a black suit jacket. It was almost as if she were trying to dress up just to bring him bad news.

Silence.

She sat behind her desk and wrestled a few papers around. "Listen, I'm making a lot of progress with Ace. He's doing better now. Working easily with children his age and not busying himself with adult issues."

"Adult issues?"

"Yes, for some reason Ace feels the need to be in charge. And a child that young shouldn't have to worry about such things. Don't you agree?"

"Let me guess, you are about to tell me that you won't approve his release." He paused. "Is that it?"

"Yes." She closed the folder on her desk. "I'm afraid I can't release him at this time."

"Why?"

She was frightened about the threat Zantonio leveled. In the end, she was scared of the wrong man.

"I understand that you really —."

"You would do this after everything I've said?" Banks questioned. "After all of my warnings?"

"Mr. Wales, all I'm asking for is a little more time with Ace. That way he can be even more —."

"Time is up."

Banks rose slowly, exited her office, and looked back once.

RIVER

River was pining through a bunch of papers on her dining room table. When Tinsley walked into the living room, he paused and looked at the array before him. "What's all this?"

"Nothing."

He frowned. "River, let's not start doing that shit again."

She sighed. "Okay, I'm trying to see what I can do to have a well-being check done on Mason."

She shook her head. "This is crazy."

"What you talking about?"

"Why are you so dead set on being in this man's marriage? The woman said she doesn't want him to see—."

River slammed her palm flat on the top of the table, scaring the fuck out of Tinsley in the process. "If it were you in that house, and someone unstable was taking care of you, you would want everybody and their mother's uncle to get involved. You heard Anita with your own ears!"

He looked down. "I'm sorry. You're right."

"If he tells me he's fine and doesn't need my help and I can see it in his eyes, I will back off. I swear I will. But if I get any idea that he isn't safe, I..."

"You what?"

"I don't know what I might do. This man is like a father to me. And I want him to know that betting on me, that saving my life was not a mistake. I've done so much shit, Tin. I just want to set some things right."

"You did so much shit like what, River? What are you talking about? I'm—."

BANG! BANG! BANG!

They both looked at the door.

"Open up! It's the police!"

River jumped up and Tinsley froze in place.

As the police continued to pound on the door, they knew this was the moment where Tinsley's life would be forever changed.

River quickly rushed up to him and looked into his eyes. This would be the hardest thing she ever had to do; she was certain.

BANG! BANG! BANG!

"It's the police! Don't make us break this door down!"

River looked down at him, snaked her hand in the back of his head and whispered in his ear. "It was me. I killed your ex-boyfriend Benji." Slowly she removed her hand from his head. "I'm so sorry. I thought he was going to hurt you and I was trying to protect you."

"This is…this is your fault?"

She nodded yes. "And I'll tell them right now so—."

The door came crashing down as armed police officers laid both River and Tinsley face down on the floor. As law enforcement flooded their home, reality hit. From their positions they were able to look into each other's eyes.

"Tinsley Adams, you are being charged with the murder of Benji Cohen," one of the officers said.

Tears rolled sideways down Tinsley's face as he continued to look at River.

"I'll tell them it was me," she whispered as she watched them handcuff him. "Just—."

"No," he mouthed as he cried harder. "Don't."

They yanked him up and pulled him out of the house.

ZERCY

Zantonio stood over his parents' graves as he held onto a bottle of Hennessey. Half of it was gone but it was evident that he had full intentions on finishing the rest.

When Zercy approached Zantonio took a large swig and shook his head. "I thought you didn't like gravesites."

"I don't." He focused on the headstone.

"So, what you doing here?"

"It's the anniversary of their deaths." Zercy said.

"How you know I was here?"

"I guessed." He paused. "I come every year about the time they died." Zercy paused. "But I never saw you here before. It was usually me and...and..."

"Our sisters!" Zantonio yelled. "You filled with so much guilt you can't even say their fucking names." He shook his head. "You know, I heard the Wales and Lou families were trouble, but I never thought this shit would end up on our doorstep." He took another swig as alcohol squirmed down his mouth. "I was wrong."

"I'm sorry, man," Zercy said as tears rolled down his cheek. "But what did you think would happen? You started a war just to get back at me. For the triplets. Wrong move. You underestimated your opponent."

"It wasn't just about you."

Zercy shook his head. "I never wanted anything to happen to you or the girls. I tried to warn them. I tried to warn you too. Banks Wales is dangerous, and nothing will stop him from getting what he wants. He's so focused he would kill himself if he got in the way of his own plans."

"You sound like a fan."

"At least I know where he's coming from."

"He killed both of them." Zantonio cried. "All three of our sisters! Gone! What the fuck! Our entire family is wiped out. But us. And you singing his praises?"

"I know and I'm so sorry about this too." He released the hammer in the back of his pants.

Zantonio swayed but maintained his footing. "So, this is how it's going down?"

"I wanted to do this myself. I wanted the last face you see to be someone you loved."

"Do it yourself?" He repeated. "You foul as fuck!"

"Your own men, who you thought were on your side, betrayed you twice. First when they took Banks' money to return Minnesota."

"And the second time?"

"When they told me where you were today. Money turns niggas."

"So, you going to betray me too?"

"No. I'm going to kill you." He fired into his chest. The liquor bottle crashed to the stone. "I'm sorry, brother." He watched him close his eyes. "I'm sorry."

When he took his last breath, he removed his cell phone from his pocket and rose. Dialing Banks' number, he said, "Its done. Can I see Minnesota now?"

Dr. Holman rushed into the house and toward her bedroom to pack a bag. The plan was to catch an eight o'clock flight to Hawaii. But when she turned left, she saw someone in her home she wasn't expecting to see.

Munro.

He was sitting in the corner of the room, on the floor waiting. Slowly he rose and aimed a weapon in her direction.

"Please, please don't," she said extending her palms. "I can let Ace go now. I...I...um...I—."

"You heard the boss. Time is up." He raised the barrel and shot her head on.

She died instantly.

CHAPTER TWENTY-TWO

HAPPY ENDINGS

Minnesota was sitting in one of the rooms inside of the Safe House. She was the first one there and more were on the way.

Although Banks said he wouldn't force her to go to the island, he wasn't willing to leave her without security until he was certain she would be protected, even after he left.

But the loneliness was killing her.

Not only because she was surrounded by security outside of her door and around the house, but she missed one person in particular. Someone that due to the circumstances, she was certain she would never see again.

But when the door opened and she saw Zercy led in by two men, while he was wearing a blindfold, she jumped up.

They walked out, leaving the two alone.

Snatching the blindfold off his eyes she squeezed him in relief.

She wasn't the only person who was relieved and pleased. Because it wasn't until that moment that he realized that she wanted him too. That she was still in love.

"They covered my eyes because they—."

"They didn't want you to know where the house is." She paused. "Once again my father is being overprotective."

"I thought he was doing too much at first. But I get him now. I swear I do."

"This is unreal," she kissed him. "I can't believe he brought you here." She kissed his lips and cheeks again.

She didn't stop until every ounce of his face had been touched.

Smiling he said, "You don't know how good it feels to fucking see you, Minnie. I was so worried."

She was about to kiss him again until she saw his eyes. They were the eyes of a man who lost it all and had nothing left to lose.

Grabbing his hand, she walked him to the side of the bed. "What happened, Zercy? Tell me everything."

In that moment he told her all he had endured. Losing all of his siblings. Two by his hands and learning that they were absolutely responsible for his parents' death as well as the death of his old girlfriend.

In the end he had come clean with it all and she did her best to be there for him in his hour of need. "I'm so sorry, Zercy."

He sighed. "Me too. I...I lost my way." He shook his head slowly from left to right. "And now all I wanna do is get back. Get back to the man I once was despite knowing that it won't be easy."

She grabbed his hand and squeezed. "And I'm going to be with you every step of the way."

"Every step?"

She smiled. "Yes, Zercy."

"Meaning like, you won't leave me?"

She shook her head. "I'm not going anywhere."

"Good, because if we're going to be in paradise together, I at least want us to be able to talk to one another."

She released his hand and covered her lips. "Wait, you're...you're going?"

He winked.

"Zercy, don't play with me."

"Mr. Wales said he wants you to be safe. And the only way he can guarantee that was if I was with you on that island."

Minnesota wrapped her arms around him and cried tears of joy. Things felt so right.

But she was a Wales, I tell you.

And Wales members never had happy endings!

THE SAFE HOUSE

The safehouse was a secure work of art. Hidden in an undisclosed location, every window was bulletproof and had bars on the glass. Banks also had ten of the best armed guards' money could buy protecting the property. And they were prepared to defend the family with their lives.

The only way in the house was through the front door, and two of his best covered that entry point.

When Spacey rushed into the safe house after being told the one thing he didn't want to hear, he was ready to fight.

Rushing past the new generation, Walid, Blakeslee, Riot and Patrick, he moved deeper into the bunker until he happened upon Minnesota's quarters.

Opening the door without knocking, he was angry to see Zercy laying in the bed.

Slamming the door like a jilted lover, he said, "Fuck is you doing, Minnesota?" He yelled. "Why is he even in here."

She giggled. "What are you talking about? We waiting for our ride to get on the jet. Where's dad?"

"Making arrangements for Ace!" He frowned. "And here you are posted up in the bed like a slut!"

"Hold up," Zercy yelled.

"You hold the fuck up! What are you doing here?"

"What it look like, man? Spending time with my girl before we leave. Why you wilding?"

"You can't go with us," Spacey said shaking his head.

"I think you are mistaken. Your father already gave me the okay."

Spacey felt the room was spinning. He had known his father to be smart. So why would he make such a bad move as to invite a stranger to paradise?

Spacey, so angry he couldn't breathe, reached behind himself. He was about to pull his gun and make the bed wet with blood, knowing that Banks would forgive him with time and apologies until Minnesota said, "If you do that, I will never forgive you. Ever. It's not a game, Spacey."

Spacey's jaw twitched.

"What's going on?" Zercy asked, clueless that he was almost a dead man.

The moment was shared between siblings.

"This is a mistake," Spacey said. "And I don't give a fuck no more. You can't—."

Suddenly his phone rang. He removed it instead of his pistol. "What?" He answered.

"It's Arman."

Spacey glared. Because he was the one who shot at Minnesota at his behest, his heart dropped.

Fuck was he calling him for?

Stepping away a little he whispered, "What you want?"

"You not safe in that house."

He glared. "Hold up, you threatening me?"

"The streets on the way."

"First off, this place is off the grid."

"Trust me, somebody dropped the ball in your camp. I don't know who it is, but my information is solid. You may live in Rich World, but I still breathe the streets."

"Why you telling me this?"

"You forgot what you said already? That it's my job to remind you every day of my fucking life that what we did together won't come back. Well, this is my way of doing it."

Spacey stuffed his phone in his pocket as his mind turned. Who could've did them wrong? And then he glanced over at Zercy's ass.

All posted up like he owned the bitch.

Removing his weapon from his pocket he said, "So you a fucking snake?"

"What are you doing now?" Minnesota yelled.

"This nigga told the streets where we were."

"What? No, I didn't!" He jumped out of bed.

"Then how come we have niggas on the way right now to snatch us. Probably for ransom?"

Minnesota eased out of bed holding her stomach. "What are you talking about?"

"I'm talking about you bedded a traitor. I told you he would betray us!" He looked at Zercy. "I thought you were all in love, nigga."

"Listen, I don't know a lot but when it comes to this woman, I would lay down my life for her!"

Minnesota thought for a moment. "Where is your phone?"

"Your father took it before he let me in. I was dropped off, remember? And don't forget they blindfolded me all the way here. I don't even know where we are."

"What's going on?" Spacey asked.

"In the past, his sisters tapped his phone. So, I figured they could do it again."

Spacey glared "He could still be tracked. Are you wearing the same clothes you were wearing the last time you saw your people?"

Zercy thought about when he was knocked out at the park. "Yeah."

"Get undressed."

"Spacey, if you wanna see his dick just say so."

"Don't fucking play with me!" Spacey snapped at her before focusing back on Zercy. "Get undressed, nigga. Now!"

Embarrassed, Zercy removed all his clothing except his sneaks and boxers.

"I said everything."

Minnesota wanted to die.

Zercy removed his boxers and a dick so big plopped out that because of seeing it, Spacey would have a complex for the rest of his life.

"Satisfied?" Zercy said raising his hands.

"The shoes too." Spacey said, maintaining his aim.

He kicked them off and Minnesota went through them. Within two minutes they found a tracker on the flap of the tongue of his tennis shoes.

All three were shocked.

"They must've put it there when they knocked me out."

Spacey tucked his gun in his back. "We got to get the kids to the lock room. And then grab the guns out the safe. I'll alert security."

But it was too late.

They wasted too much time.

And as a result, the goons of Baltimore had already snuffed out three of the ten guards. And within minutes they took out five more. After all, they were twenty deep and Banks' killers simply weren't enough.

Approaching the two men at the door, Shopper, with the bad eye that looked like it was covered by white silk said, "Now we getting in that house." He looked back at his nineteen men. "You can either die a noble death or you can go home to be with your family. But understand, nothing gonna stop us from getting that paper."

"Don't you mean people?"

"Same thing," Shopper laughed.

It seemed like forever, but the two remaining guards looked at one another and fired at the goons.

For their efforts, both dropped at the door. Dead at work. Multiple bullets in their chest cavities.

They went out with honor, but their families wouldn't see it that way.

Walking inside, they were prepared to collect as many Wales as possible for profit when they saw Spacey, Minnesota and Zercy aiming their way.

"No need to fret. We just want two Wales. A little one and the girl right there since they share Banks' bloodline. The way we see it, ya'll should be worth a million apiece." Shopper laughed. "So, give them to —."

Minnesota shot him in the center of the head.

His big body dropped.

She was so quick that it stunned everyone present.

The remaining Baltimore Goons knew at that moment everyone would not make it out alive. But they reasoned that they would probably die for free on the streets of Baltimore anyway.

Wasn't it worth it to risk everything for a chance at millions?

And so, they advanced forward slowly.

It was over.

The Wales and friend were outnumbered.

Minnesota looked at Spacey and said, "I love you."

"I love you too," he mouthed.

She focused on Zercy who kissed her lips.

With that they started firing.

They hit a few on the shoulders and chin or whatever, but it simply wasn't enough.

But then something happened.

The men in the back started to run, as gunfire sounded off in the distance. Consumed, most of the goons started to flee only to be met with a machine gun's death.

"Is that Dad?" Minnesota asked, shocked at the turn of events.

"I don't think so!" Spacey's heart thumped wildly. "He's busy with trying to arrange the escape. I wasn't able to get him on the phone. I was supposed to meet up with him and Joey later."

When they walked outside, slowly, stepping over the corpses in the process, they saw a sea of bodies. In the back was Arman and his eight men.

Spacey balled over laughing as he looked at the man, he was sure at one time was going to get him caught up.

"What's funny?" Arman asked.

"You just became one of the richest niggas in Maryland."

"I'll take that!" He smiled.

Ten minutes later, the scheduled luxury mobile home arrived and everyone, including the kids piled inside. Spacey was finally able to get a hold of Banks, who saw to it that Arman's millions were taken to a place of his choosing.

Missing death again, the family drove out of sight.

But danger was a persistent bitch.

And it craved Wales' blood.

BANKS

Banks and Joey were standing in the dining room of Banks' mansion staring at the cell phone. After what seemed like forever, it finally rang.

Slowly Banks picked up the handset. "Yes."

Joey waited impatiently for the word.

"Thanks," Banks continued.

When he hung up Joey asked, "We good?"

Banks nodded. "It's time."

Ace sat at his desk in his bedroom.

He wasn't sure but something about the energy felt different. And as a result, he was a bit on edge. When the door opened and a woman he'd seen before from afar walked inside, he rose.

She was carrying a glass of apple juice. Ace's favorite.

"I want my father," he said.

She smiled and placed the juice on the table. "Drink all of it."

"Why?"

"Because I asked you to."

"My dad says I don't have to do anything I don't want to do. And I don't want to drink it."

"If you drink this, you'll be free."

"What that mean?"

"Drink it and you'll go home."

Quickly he grabbed the juice and drank every drop. When he was done, she snatched the glass and walked out of the room.

A few minutes later he held his little stomach. Before long, he vomited on the floor. When he tried to sit down, he vomited again. The juice had ipecac syrup which although no longer available in stores, could still be obtained on the dark market.

Rushing out of his room he moved toward the first adult to get his attention. "I'm sick."

"You're not going home, Ace. Stop faking like you always do. It's—."

He vomited on his shoes.

Taking the boy seriously, he ushered him quickly to the nurse's office.

"What's wrong with him now?" Nurse Lowan asked the Residential Assistant.

"He's sick."

"Ace is always faking like something is wrong with him. Give him some ginger ale and —."

He vomited again, stopping all conversation. Now she also believed the boy who was often a little liar. Which was the purpose of the syrup all along.

"Sit him on the bed," she directed. "Quick. I'll get his vitals."

As she checked his temperature and the like within seconds the fire alarms blared everywhere.

"What's going on now?" Nurse Lowan asked, eyes still on the wealthiest child in the facility.

"I don't know. But I'll be right back. Keep an eye on him." He ran out of the office.

Banks' ex-best friend Joanne was in the mobile home helping get the children together for the flight. Ever since they reunited, she did all she could to help Banks live out his dream of getting out of the states and living in paradise.

With the meals for Blakeslee, Ace, Walid, Patrick, and Riot prepared, she lined everything up on the counter when Morgan called *The Family Cell*. A secure line Banks set up for his most trusted.

"Can I talk to Banks?" Morgan asked. "Alone?"

"He's working on getting Ace and —."

"Please," she continued. "I know you are going to talk to him at some point tonight. I don't know what the plan is, but I can tell you're involved. Just, just let him know that I want to go. That I'm willing to give it all up to be with the kids. To help raise them."

"You would leave everything?"

"To retire in paradise?" She paused. "In a heartbeat."

The Children's Home for Troubled Boys was mostly up in flames.

Suddenly the backdoor flew open, and Ace was escorted out by two men. One on the right and the other on his left. Each was armed and ready for war if one hair was harmed on the royal boy's head.

They had taken the boy out of the nurse's office and so far, things were going as planned.

Banks would be proud.

There was so much fire and smoke, that the scene behind the young prince was reminiscent of a music video.

But this wasn't for entertainment purposes.

This was to cause a diversion that would get Ace out safely and it looked like it worked.

Once outside, the door to the black van slid open and Ace was placed inside. The moment his seatbelt was buckled, and a diamond medallion chain was dropped around his neck he grinned.

The two hitters sat next to the boy for his utmost protection. Their only job in life was to get that boy to the next destination.

Joey, who was in the driver's seat looked back at his kid brother. "You good back there, lil bro?"

"I am now." He ran his fingertips over his jewels. The stones were as cool as ice to his touch.

"Good, because we out."

Joey smiled and pulled away from the facility at a high speed. Everything seemed to be going as planned and then, suddenly, a police cruiser pulled behind them with flashing red and blue lights.

"Fuck!" He slapped at the steering wheel.

"Make sure Ace is good back there!" He directed the hitters. "I'm gonna try to shake them off our trail."

"We got him!" Nathaniel responded.

Joey hooked a left and still the cop was on his heels. He turned right, slamming into the side of a trash can and still the cop remained.

He was pushing the limit as safely as possible in an attempt to escape. But he wasn't able to get rid of him. It was obvious that the officer knew what he was doing. He was also certain that in a matter of moments, more cops would flood the block.

"I want my father," Ace said getting scared about the rough motion of the vehicle.

"I know, lil man," Joey said continuing to pilot the van aggressively. "I got you though. Trust me. I won't let anything happen to you."

Just that quickly his brother, Harris, entered his mind.

This wasn't the first time Banks attempted to free a son. Back in the day he tried to break Harris out of jail. It was a tragedy that resulted in Harris dying due to a stab wound. Which was also Banks' plan gone wrong.

Would he fail at freeing Ace too?

Joey was just about to give up when a vehicle came from left field and slammed into the police cruiser. After being struck, the car spiraled sideways and landed upside down.

"Oh shit!" Joey yelled as he continued to handle the van while looking at the crash from his rearview mirror.

When the vehicle responsible for the accident pulled alongside him, he saw his father was in the passenger seat with Munro driving.

"Meet me at the other spot!" Banks ordered pointing ahead.

Joey grinned. "I'm on my way!"

Banks winked.

The wooded area was thick and yet in the center was a road which held a luxury mobile home. Munro drove into the hidden path with Joey following close behind. In the distance police sirens could be heard and all knew they were searching for Ace and the person responsible for crashing into a police cruiser.

Once parked, Banks exited his car.

While Joey and Ace stepped out of the van.

The moment Banks was in front of Ace, he picked him up and held him into his arms. It felt like forever.

Grabbing at the chain on his neck he said, "You looking good."

Ace wrapped his arms around his neck again. "I'm back." Banks chuckled because Ace stayed with the quips.

Placing Ace down, he walked up to Joey and hugged him too. "Good job."

"Thanks, Pops."

When the chivalries were over, they approached the mobile home which was covered by armed men.

The moment Banks opened the doors, he smiled at all the children playing happily inside. There was Blakeslee, Patrick, Walid and Riot.

The moment Walid saw his brother, he rushed up to him and pulled him into a tight hug. It was the type of embrace that rocked everybody's hearts onboard. Not only because it was apparent how much they loved one another, but it was obvious how much they missed each other too.

Reunited, the two bopped into the back of the mobile home and kept time, doing their best to catch up.

Twin faces.

Different hearts.

Also in attendance were Joanne, Munro, Minnesota, Zercy, Spacey, a nurse and Morgan, who Banks had given the okay earlier in the day to go with them on the island. He was relieved that Morgan wanted to go because it meant he would have yet another person he trusted around.

Joanne walked up to him. "Everything is ready for the ride to the jet."

"You sure you don't wanna come with me?"

She rose on her tiptoes and kissed him on the lips. "I wish I could. Goodbye old friend."

"Goodbye." He said as Munro helped her off.

Walking up to his most trusted man, he placed a hand on his shoulder. "You've been loyal, Munro. I wouldn't—."

"I'm going to see you to the jet, sir. Safely. If you don't mind. We can say our goodbyes then."

Banks nodded and smiled.

Munro took a seat.

Although most of the passengers were happy to be one step closer to paradise, Spacey had an attitude.

"You good?" Banks asked him seeing his sour mood.

Spacey looked back at Zercy and then him. "I guess."

"Is everybody here?" He asked Spacey.

"Nah. Not everybody." Spacey cleared his throat and looked away.

Banks reassessed the passengers again and this time noticed Sidney was missing. Turning around he said, "Where is your wife, son?" He asked Joey.

He looked down. "I'm not going, Pops."

He frowned. "What? Why not?"

Having heard her brother's response, Minnesota rushed up to him. "What are you doing? Why aren't you coming with us?"

"Come on, brother," Spacey said standing up. "Don't do this shit!"

"She doesn't wanna go, man. And I, I can't leave my wife here."

"Fuck!" Spacey yelled before flopping back in his seat. He felt like smacking the hell out of his sister-in-law. "You staying for a bitch!"

"Don't disrespect your brother!" Banks yelled.

"Exactly!" Joey shouted.

"Are you sure?" He asked focusing back on Joey.

He nodded. "I am."

Minnesota hugged Joey and walked away, to prevent crying.

Banks stepped closer to Joey and then stepped back. For the first time in months, he removed his shades and looked him in the eyes. "I don't want you to stay here. Let me talk to Sidney. Maybe I can —."

"Pops, I can't. I been trying all night. She doesn't want to go, and I want to respect her reasons."

Banks took a deep breath, snaked his hand behind the back of his head and placed his forehead against Joey's. "Thank you. For everything." He looked him into the eyes. "I love you, son."

Their foreheads still connected.

"I love you too."

"And I remember you. I remember everything. Even when you were a baby and I watched you come into this world."

Joey wrapped his arms around his body, and they embraced. It was long and heartfelt as he cried in his arms.

After releasing tears and wiping them away with two fists to the face, Joey stepped off the mobile home.

The doors closed and the vehicle slowly pulled away.

"Don't worry, boss," Munro said. "I'll look after him."

Fucked up that one of his sons were left behind, Banks plopped in his seat and took a deep breath before Spacey sat next to him. The smell of smoke was heavy on Banks, Ace and the guards clothing.

"You okay?" Spacey asked.

Banks nodded.

"Joey will be fine, Pops."

"I'm gonna make a few calls to make sure." He sat deeper into his seat, before checking his watch. In under an hour and a half, if all went well, they would be taking flight.

Time was ticking.

"I know you will," Spacey said.

"He should've come, because I'm serious when I say, we're never coming back here. When we get on that plane tonight, that's the last time we will be in the states. Ever."

Ace and Walid laughed heavily in the background, as they told each other stories.

Spacey leaned closer. "Why you let Zercy come?"

Banks wiped his hand down his face. "Because she was going to stay too. And if she did, all of this would be for nothing."

Spacey shook his head in disagreement and Banks noticed. "Son, listen, whatever you and Minnesota had is over."

"You know about that?"

"Yeah." Banks was so disgusted he wanted to vomit. "And I don't understand what would make you see her that way, but it can't happen ever again. Are we clear?"

He nodded yes.

Banks sighed and pulled out his phone and texted a number.

"It was a strange time in my life. You don't know what they put us through in that attic, Pops."

Banks nodded. "I hear you." He leaned over. "But did you hear me too?"

Spacey sat back and sighed. "I hear you. I...I really do."

Suddenly a shiny black Maybach pulled alongside the mobile home. Highly concerned, Spacey reached for the gun in his hip until Banks pressed down heavily on his hand.

"Who is that?"

"It's my ride. I gotta make a stop."

"Pops, no! Too many police are out looking. Plus, we don't have much time!"

"Trust me. Go straight to the private hanger."

"Pull over, Pete," Banks told the driver.

"Yes, sir." He merged to the right.

"Pops, where you going though? You gotta tell me something."

Banks turned around and faced him. "Stay with the family. If anything happens, do what you gotta do to get everyone on that jet. Even if it means leaving me."

"I won't do that!" Spacey yelled, causing everyone to take notice.

Banks rushed up to him. "That's an order!" He roared. "If I don't make it back in time, take flight without me! Do you understand?"

Silence.

"Do you understand me!"

Spacey swallowed the lump in his throat and with a broken heart said, "Yes."

Banks hopped off, with Munro at his side.

They jumped in the car which was waiting.

CHAPTER TWENTY-THREE

FOUL FISH

As she sat at the dining room table feasting, Dasher was on her eighth piece of shrimp and counting. She had so much sauce on her fingertips that the shrimp almost slipped out and fell on the floor.

Over the past few days, Mason long since stopped coming to the dining room.

Besides, she had gotten so disgusting that she took to only feeding him what she didn't feel like eating. Or, if she wanted to be extra gross, she chewed up the food in her mouth as if he were a baby and spit it into his as if he were a bird.

He was miserable.

And that night, he promised that he would stab her when she was sleep, crawl his way to the phone for help, and have the baby rescued.

Whatever happened to him for committing murder he didn't care about. He was done with being her victim, but not before taking her with him.

DING DONG.

Her eyes widened and she sucked her fingers. "What the fuck?" She pushed back in the chair and slid her dirty black feet across the floor as she worked her way to the door. "Whoever it is better not wake up my baby!"

Looking out the peephole, she farted when she saw Banks on the other side. "What do you want?"

"You said I could come back any time." Banks said. "I'm here. Now open the door," he replied in a relaxed tone.

"I'm calling the police!" She threatened. "Do you hear me? I'm calling the police!"

Silence.

"Get out of here or —."

Unfortunately for her, the door came crashing down on her face as her back slammed into the floor. In that moment Banks' men flooded the house, as Banks kicked the door off her to help her to her feet.

On the way over in the Maybach, he dispatched a car full of niggas just in case he had to burn that bitch down.

"It smells like fish in this bitch," Banks said.

"Fuck you!" She yelled wiping blood off her nose and mouth. It continued to pour everywhere.

"Find him," he ordered his men. "This time look everywhere. Even if you have to tear this bitch down in the process. Floors too!"

"Sure thing, boss!" Munro said.

As they moved through the house she trembled. "I hate you." Blood splattered from her nose and dripped on the floor.

"I'm taking him with me."

"He won't go with you! He loves his wife! He won't leave his family."

"Why this house smell like seafood?"

"I won't let you have him!"

"You a nasty bitch. I can't see how he chose you to begin with."

"You jealous or something?"

Banks chuckled once. "You can never stand next to what I mean to him. But you know that already, don't you?" He grinned.

"I will call the—."

"Got him!"

The moment Banks saw Mason his heart sunk.

To say he was in a bad way was an understatement. His eyes were sunken due to malnutrition and his legs were so small even if he wanted to walk, he wouldn't be able to stand up for long.

Banks was so angry at the condition of his old friend that his legs trembled. Looking at her, Banks stepped closer and stole her in the face.

She remained on the floor where she pissed in her pajama pants.

"What you doing here, Banks?" Mason asked glaring. While, trying to pretend he didn't give a fuck about him being there even though his expression said different.

Banks' presence was literally a breath of fresh air.

"You coming with me." Banks said plainly, wiping blood off his hand.

"Where?"

"Does it matter?"

It didn't.

They both knew it.

"Th…thank you." Was all Mason could say before a flood of tears that he had been holding back released. "Thank you for not leaving me, man. Thank you…."

Some may have considered his emotions weak, but in that moment, he went from feeling as if he had no one left in the world, to being rescued by the one person on earth he ever really cared about.

"Get the baby too," Banks directed his men as they all moved toward the exit.

"You're not taking my fucking baby!" She popped up and ran behind Banks as Mason was being pushed out in his wheelchair. "Do you hear me?"

Banks shoved her back with a full palm to the face as Bolt was being held by his most trusted soldier, Munro.

Disgusted, Banks wiped the blood off his hands onto her shirt.

"Give me my baby!" She yelled, slapping his muscular back. "Give him to me you big, bitch! Give me my child!"

Banks slipped into the backseat of his Maybach as Mason was placed next to him.

"Do you hear me! " She yelled at Munro. "You aren't taking my baby!"

The thing was the baby *was* being taken and sat on Munro's lap who was in the front seat. And there wasn't shit she could do about it but scream.

Hell would freeze over before Banks would allow the same harm to come to the boy that came to his friend.

As the car pulled out in the middle of the road, Dasher continued to scream barefoot as she took off running behind the car. "GIVE ME MY BABY!"

It was too late; they were gone up the street.

And unfortunately for her, a man driving a delivery truck had looked down to pick up his phone.

When he raised his head, her body met his grill face first.

Killing her instantly.

Banks and Mason were quiet as they were driven down the road.

"You stink like fish, nigga," Banks said, breaking silence first. "Fuck were ya'll doing in that house? Eating seafood every day?"

Mason shook his head remembering the hell he had just been in. "What made you come back?"

"Does it matter?"

"No, but I wanna know."

Banks sunk deeper in his seat. Rubbing the palms of his hands on his pants he said, "I ain't trust her. Never did."

"What does that mean?"

"I'm leaving, Mason." He said seriously while also skipping the subject. "When I'm gone, I'm not coming back. And I didn't, I mean, I wanted to tell you before I bounced."

Mason nodded.

However, based on the news he would have preferred to die than to discover that he would never see his friend again.

"And if you want...if you want to come with me, you can." He looked at him. "Do you want to come?"

Mason once again felt the world rise in his honor. "I mean, I ain't got nothing left here."

"Is that a yes?"

The smile on Mason's gaunt face said it all. "Yeah. I'm rolling with you."

Banks nodded and looked at his watch. "Good. But first I have to make one more stop."

River had paperwork scattered on the table. She was wearing grey sweats and a white t-shirt soiled with whatever was around because she wore it for three days straight.

On one half of the table were documents necessary to get Tinsley the best lawyer money could buy. And when she got the bill, she learned that is exactly what she was going to have to do.

Paying for his defense meant tapping at her nest egg and her having to hit the streets again. But he was in prison for her crime and so she would do whatever it took.

But on the other side of the table were stacks of money to help Mason. She tried to play nice with Dasher in the beginning. In the end she realized his wife alone held the power and so, outside of busting in the woman's crib under the cover of night, there was nothing else she could do.

She decided to go with violence.

Using the money, she planned to pay five hard hitting men to kick the door down and find Mason.

No matter what she would see Mason's face before the sun rose.

She was just about to make a few runs and pay her hitters when the doorbell rang. Grabbing the gun on her chair, she walked carefully toward it. Who she saw on the other end almost brought her to her knees.

It was Mason Louisville.

Opening the door, she bent down and hugged him so hard he whenced in pain. And still she didn't let him go.

Finally releasing him, she said, "How did you get here?" She looked up and down the hall.

"Banks."

Her eyebrows rose. "Banks? He...he brought you?" She was beyond shocked.

"Can I come in?"

"Yes, of course." She rolled him into the living room and sat across from him on the sofa.

"I wanted to see you before I left, kid."

"Whe...where you going?"

"I don't have the exact details. Banks is taking me somewhere and it was, well, it was his idea to stop here first."

"Why?"

"I heard about how you pressed him. How you wanted to make sure I was okay. And I can see by the murder stacks on the table that your work wasn't done."

Tears welled up in her eyes. "I didn't want to hurt her. But if she wasn't going to let me in the house tonight...it was going to be whatever. I gotta be honest."

He nodded. "Listen, kid, I just, I just wanted you to know that I will never forget your loyalty. I will never forget all you put on the line for me. You are the daughter I never had and I'm so, I'm so proud of you."

River wiped her tears away roughly. "I would do anything for you."

"I know, kid." He sighed deeply. "We have to leave but I left something in the building where we held the weapons. The one Lightman fucked that dude in that night and got caught."

River laughed. "How can I forget? The nigga kept yelling, *'we were wrestling'*."

"It's in the bathroom floor. Get it tonight. I don't want the vultures coming when they find out I'm gone. I gotta go."

They embraced again and she released him.

Holding back tears she pushed him toward the door, where Banks was waiting outside the apartment with two armed men.

"Thank you for doing this," she said to him.

He nodded and pushed him to the elevator and out of sight.

Later on, that night River went to the location. Slowly she walked around back and into the room leading into the basement.

Hooking a left, she entered the small bathroom and pulled up three of the five slats on the floor.

There, hidden, were three bags.

Inside of them were five million dollars in cash.

She fell backwards.

That quickly she was back up.

It didn't look like Mason and Banks would make it to the Jet as the Maybach sped down the freeway toward the hanger.

15 minutes until flight....

The sad part is, the streets had gotten word that he was leaving that night, and all the snakes slithered quickly toward the location, for one last effort to snatch Banks and his family for profit.

Ten minutes until flight…

As the Benz offspring sped down the highway, almost defying the laws of gravity, Banks looked at Mason knowing that it was a great possibility, that they would be dead before sunrise.

Five minutes until flight.

And all they could think of was that for two kids from Baltimore, they had a hell of a ride.

A baby blue sky with fluffy clouds provided the perfect backdrop for the ten-million-dollar jet that glided through its center like a bowling ball on a freshly oiled lane. Inside the massive luxurious aircraft, scared to death, sat the passengers.

They smelled of foul fish, smoke, and despair.

And none of the passengers, not a one, was certain that they would make it to paradise. Besides, most of them didn't deserve the classic happily ever after. After all, some had killed.

Lied.

And even manipulated to get what they wanted. But when I tell you karma touched each one of their lives, believe me that it did.

Banks was faced with not being able to continue hormone therapy.

Mason was faced with not ever being able to walk, and he also lost all of his older sons.

Spacey lost Minnesota, the only thing he really wanted.

And Minnesota was bleeding in the back of the jet, which she would later discover was a miscarriage.

Prior to that, for twenty-four days they were hunted.

They were plucked off.

Only to realize that they would never be able to return to their birthplace ever again.

Propped in lavish seats, as they scanned one another's faces, their hearts pumped wildly inside of their chests. On the aircraft, they were the only people alive who knew what it meant to make the escape.

As a result, if someone shot down the plane it would be over for their legacies.

But it was in God's hands now.

And the only thing left to do was hope that their fearless leader would get them safely to the destination.

While most knowing the odds were against them.

Banks looked across the aisle at his best friend who was staring his way. Mason being there was not in the plan, and yet there they were, two old friends leaving a place they would never return.

But it made the most sense.

Because as the world came down around them, per usual, at least they had one another.

Mason looked at their children on the plane and back at Banks. He was grinning from ear to ear.

"What, nigga?" Banks snapped. "Why you looking so goofy?"

"You don't remember, do you?"

"I remember you fucking up three sandwiches in under an hour."

"Nah, I'm talking about when we were kids. And you told me the plan."

Banks sat deeper in the chair. "I don't remember. How about you tell me."

WHEN THEY WERE YOUNG

Banks and Mason were on a Ferris wheel at a carnival when suddenly it stopped, putting the two at the very top.

Mason was on edge but Banks, who already developed a desire to fly away, felt on top of the world. He smiled as he was able to see everything from afar.

He was in his element.

If only his friend wasn't so nervous, it could've been a pleasant memory. But the homie was so scared he was about to cry.

Mason's nervousness put Banks on pause. He was used to him playing so tough. He reasoned that everyone had a fear. And for Mason it was heights.

Trying to make him feel better, Banks scooted closer and remove a piece of paper from his pocket. Unfolding the document, it revealed a design of the earlier stages of his island. Something that he obsessed over every day of his young life.

"What you doing?" Mason yelled. "I don't wanna see that shit! I want to get off here."

"This where I'm gonna live when I get older," Banks said calmly.

The thing was, Mason wasn't interested in his drawing. What he wanted to do was faint. "I want to get out!" He yelled. "I want to go home! Help! Help!"

"Look, man," Banks pointed to the paper again. "I'm gonna live here and you gonna be here too."

Now he had Mason's attention.

Because Banks, as a boy, never talked about them being together. Besides, he had his crush and so Mason was never in the picture. So, hearing those words caused Mason's heart to jump.

"What's gonna be there?"

"Trees. The beach. Oh, we gonna have so much money we can eat what we want. And, and do what we want."

"And kids? Like, me and yours?"

Banks couldn't see that happening, but he wanted his friend to be okay.

"Yep, lots of kids. And we will live happily ever after."

"You promise?" Mason asked.

Silence.

"Do you promise, Banks?"

He smiled. "Yes, I promise."

Upon the declaration to the universe, the Ferris wheel moved.

EPILOGUE – TUESDAY

MANY YEARS LATER

The night sky was spectacular for Ace and Walid's eighteenth birthday party. Stars sparkled and the ocean sang as beautiful women with brown skin and long black flowing hair danced for their attention.

Behind the ladies sat a band, which played the twins favorite songs. They were doing the job so well; one could hardly tell the original from the cover.

It's true, Banks and Mason didn't hold back a stack when it came to ushering their spawns into adulthood.

Gone were the boys of yesteryear.

The twins had transformed and became men so exotic looking, that both sexes did double takes when witnessing their beauty.

With time's blessing, Ace and Walid had turned into tall muscular men with skin, literally the color of golden sand. Every inch of their bodies was covered in tribal tattoos and their long black curly hair was gold at the tips, healthy and shiny.

Per usual, Ace wore his mane wild and out of control while Walid preferred to tame his with a gold hair band.

Walid was muted in his clothing choices. Preferring the comfort of linen or no shirt at all.

But Ace longed for the rich, hood nigga life and the diamond chain draped around his neck that read *I AM GOD* told the world about his hidden desire for power, money, and everything in between.

They looked like stars.

And to the islanders they were.

But more things than just their bodies changed over the years.

Walid met the love of his life. A beautiful island girl who had given birth to his son, Baltimore Wales. Walid loved his family truly and had grown to become a man of honor, code and generosity.

In fact, it was whispered that his only weakness was his brother.

And unfortunately for Walid, that was the most dangerous weakness to possess.

Ace was an entirely different person all together.

If being accurate was a requirement, he would be considered a monster.

Ace was more selfish than a Pitbull being asked to share from his bowl. Meaner than a rattle snake and as sneaky as a stickup kid watching a block nigga pocket his cash after a night's work.

Sure they had the same faces.

But they didn't share the same hearts.

The only positive attribute Ace possessed was the complete love he had for his twin, even though his actions often said differently.

But tonight, it was a celebration.

For darkness was at bay.

Well, not really.

As the twins sat on gold and black throne chairs and watched a group of beautiful women dance for them in the sand, Ace sighed and sunk deeper into despair. His desire to taste blood was growing by the second.

"What's wrong, brother?" Walid asked leaning to the right. Shirtless, his muscles buckled under the moonlight.

Ace sighed. "Do you ever get tired of it all?" He readjusted his dick to the left.

"Of what?"

"Of having everything and nothing at the same time." When he saw one of the dancers gawking, he shoved his button-down shirt to the left and right, as if he was opening curtains, just to be sure his jewels shined through.

Walid looked to his left at his girlfriend who played with his son and exhaled. "Nah, I like not having to worry about anything. I like knowing that my family is safe. I'm at peace, brother. And I wish you could be too."

His girlfriend winked at her man.

He winked back.

Ace glared.

He hated when his brother sounded what he deemed as weak.

"That's because you got a girl and my nephew," he continued. "But what I got? Nothing. And I need something of my own." He focused on the only beauty amongst the dancers who refused to give him eye contact.

"You got a lot. You had a few women too, but you always cut them off when they want you to commit." He laughed. "Maybe you need adventure. Pops and Uncle Mason said we can take a trip to−."

"Another island! I'm tired of going to other islands!"

"Then were you wanna go?"

"America! Where we were born!"

Walid sat back as if he just said fighting words. "They said we would never be able to go back there. You know that. And to be honest, based on what we see on the news I don't want to. Maybe —."

"I know what they said! But I'm sick of following their rules!"

A few people paused to see what the princes were yelling about.

"But what about what we want, brother?" Ace waved one of their employees over. "Tell that girl to come over here. The one with the heart tattoo on her wrist."

"Sure boss."

When the employee whispered to the girl, she looked at Ace and shook her head. Sadly the employee approached having unfulfilled his request. "She said no. Did you want one of the other young ladies? One of them seems to be quite smitten with you. I can —."

"Do you work for her or me?" He glared up at him.

"Leave it alone, brother," Walid said.

"You know what, I'll do it myself. I be right back." Ace rose, yanked off his shirt and dropped it on the beach. Storming over to the dancers, he kicked up sand like smoke trails from speeding tires.

The I AM GOD medallion glistened against his chiseled chest.

And yet he looked like a beautiful devil.

Grabbing the girl by the arm, he yanked her over to the towel shack as they both disappeared inside.

It was caveman style.

Walid grew uneasy wondering what was going on while also knowing that in Ace's mind he could be, have and do whatever he wanted. The island was literally named, Wales Island.

And they were island princes.

So, didn't that mean they were invincible?

Ace certainly thought so.

Fifteen minutes later as the band continued to play, the beautiful island girl with the heart tattoo came running out of the shack, her clothing hanging off her arm. She was also partially covered in blood.

A few seconds later, Ace exited adjusting his linen pants. Scratches were all over his bare chest and a blood drop sat on his diamonds.

Flopping in his throne he looked over at his brother and grinned. "I'm bored, Wally. I need an escape."

"What did you do?" Walid glared.

"What I always do. Took what I wanted." He placed a heavy hand on his shoulder. "Now do your job and go clean up my mess." He winked. "I know you can never help yourself."

"Be careful with me, brother." Walid warned. "You won't get away with how you moving in life for long."

Ace winked. "I guess we gonna see."

COMING SOON

THE GOD'S OF

EVERYTHING ELSE

(An Ace & Walid Saga)

CONNECT WITH T. STYLES

WWW.TOYSTYLES.COM

WANT TO LEARN HOW TO WRITE OR PUBLISH

A BOOK?

VISIT:

WWW.THEELITEWRITERSACADEMY.COM

CARTEL PUBLICATIONS

PRESENTS

The Cartel Publications Order Form

www.thecartelpublications.com

Inmates **ONLY** receive novels for $10.00 per book **PLUS** shipping fee **PER BOOK.**

(Mail Order **MUST** come from inmate directly to receive discount)

Shyt List 1	$15.00
Shyt List 2	$15.00
Shyt List 3	$15.00
Shyt List 4	$15.00
Shyt List 5	$15.00
Shyt List 6	$15.00
Pitbulls In A Skirt	$15.00
Pitbulls In A Skirt 2	$15.00
Pitbulls In A Skirt 3	$15.00
Pitbulls In A Skirt 4	$15.00
Pitbulls In A Skirt 5	$15.00
Victoria's Secret	$15.00
Poison 1	$15.00
Poison 2	$15.00
Hell Razor Honeys	$15.00
Hell Razor Honeys 2	$15.00
A Hustler's Son	$15.00
A Hustler's Son 2	$15.00
Black and Ugly	$15.00
Black and Ugly As Ever	$15.00
Ms Wayne & The Queens of DC **(LGBT)**	$15.00
Black And The Ugliest	$15.00
Year Of The Crackmom	$15.00
Deadheads	$15.00
The Face That Launched A Thousand Bullets	$15.00
The Unusual Suspects	$15.00
Paid In Blood	$15.00
Raunchy	$15.00
Raunchy 2	$15.00
Raunchy 3	$15.00
Mad Maxxx (4th Book Raunchy Series)	$15.00
Quita's Dayscare Center	$15.00
Quita's Dayscare Center 2	$15.00
Pretty Kings	$15.00
Pretty Kings 2	$15.00
Pretty Kings 3	$15.00
Pretty Kings 4	$15.00
Silence Of The Nine	$15.00
Silence Of The Nine 2	$15.00
Silence Of The Nine 3	$15.00

Prison Throne	_____	$15.00
Drunk & Hot Girls	_____	$15.00
Hersband Material **(LGBT)**	_____	$15.00
The End: How To Write A	_____	$15.00
Bestselling Novel In 30 Days (Non-Fiction Guide)		
Upscale Kittens	_____	$15.00
Wake & Bake Boys	_____	$15.00
Young & Dumb	_____	$15.00
Young & Dumb 2: Vyce's Getback	_____	$15.00
Tranny 911 **(LGBT)**	_____	$15.00
Tranny 911: Dixie's Rise **(LGBT)**	_____	$15.00
First Comes Love, Then Comes Murder	_____	$15.00
Luxury Tax	_____	$15.00
The Lying King	_____	$15.00
Crazy Kind Of Love	_____	$15.00
Goon	_____	$15.00
And They Call Me God	_____	$15.00
The Ungrateful Bastards	_____	$15.00
Lipstick Dom **(LGBT)**	_____	$15.00
A School of Dolls **(LGBT)**	_____	$15.00
Hoetic Justice	_____	$15.00
KALI: Raunchy Relived	_____	$15.00
(5th Book in Raunchy Series)		
Skeezers	_____	$15.00
Skeezers 2	_____	$15.00
You Kissed Me, Now I Own You	_____	$15.00
Nefarious	_____	$15.00
Redbone 3: The Rise of The Fold	_____	$15.00
The Fold (4th Redbone Book)	_____	$15.00
Clown Niggas	_____	$15.00
The One You Shouldn't Trust	_____	$15.00
The WHORE The Wind		
Blew My Way	_____	$15.00
She Brings The Worst Kind	_____	$15.00
The House That Crack Built	_____	$15.00
The House That Crack Built 2	_____	$15.00
The House That Crack Built 3	_____	$15.00
The House That Crack Built 4	_____	$15.00
Level Up **(LGBT)**	_____	$15.00
Villains: It's Savage Season	_____	$15.00
Gay For My Bae	_____	$15.00
War	_____	$15.00
War 2: All Hell Breaks Loose	_____	$15.00
War 3: The Land Of The Lou's	_____	$15.00
War 4: Skull Island	_____	$15.00
War 5: Karma	_____	$15.00
War 6: Envy	_____	$15.00
War 7: Pink Cotton	_____	$15.00
Madjesty vs. Jayden (Novella)	_____	$8.99
You Left Me No Choice	_____	$15.00
Truce – A War Saga (War 8)	_____	$15.00
Ask The Streets For Mercy	_____	$15.00
Truce 2 - (War 9)	_____	$15.00
An Ace and Walid Very, Very Bad Christmas (War 10)	_____	$15.00
Truce 3 – The Sins of The Fathers (War 11)	_____	$15.00
Truce 4: The Finale (War 12)	_____	$15.00

By T. STYLES

(**Redbone 1** & **2** are **NOT** Cartel Publications novels and if **ordered** the cost is **FULL** price of $15.00 **each**. **No Exceptions**.)

Please add **$5.00** for shipping and handling fees for up to **(2) BOOKS PER ORDER**. (INMATES INCLUDED) (See next page for details)

The Cartel Publications * P.O. BOX 486 OWINGS MILLS MD 21117

Name: _____

Address: _____

City/State: _____

Contact/Email: _____

Please allow 10-15 BUSINESS days Before shipping.

PLEASE NOTE DUE TO <u>COVID-19</u> SOME ORDERS MAY TAKE UP TO <u>3 WEEKS OR LONGER</u> BEFORE THEY SHIP

The Cartel Publications is <u>NOT</u> responsible for <u>Prison Orders</u> rejected!

<u>NO RETURNS and NO REFUNDS</u>
<u>NO PERSONAL CHECKS ACCEPTED</u>
<u>STAMPS NO LONGER ACCEPTED</u>

CPSIA information can be obtained
at www.ICGtesting.com
Printed in the USA
LVHW092045170821
695490LV00001B/92

9 781948 373753